A Matched Pair: Amish Matchmaker: Book Two

Copyright © Samantha Bayarr 2019

Scripture quotations are from New King James Version of the Bible.

A NOTE FROM THE AUTHOR

While this story is set against the backdrop of an Amish community, the characters and the town are fictional. There is no intended resemblance between the characters and community in this story and any real members of the Amish or communities. As with any work of fiction, I've taken license in some areas of research as a means of creating the necessary circumstances for my characters and the community in which they live. My research and experience with the Amish are quite knowledgeable; however, it would be impossible to be entirely accurate in details and description since every community differs, and I have not lived near enough the Amish community for several years to know pertinent and current details. Therefore, any inaccuracies in the Amish lifestyle and their community portrayed in this book are due to fictional license as the author.

Thank you for being such a loyal reader.

TABLE OF CONTENTS

CHAPTER ONE

CHAPTER TWO

CHAPTER THREE

CHAPTER FOUR

CHAPTER FIVE

CHAPTER SIX

CHAPTER SEVEN

CHAPTER EIGHT

CHAPTER NINE

CHAPTER TEN

CHAPTER ELEVEN

CHAPTER TWELVE

CHAPTER THIRTEEN

CHAPTER FOURTEEN

CHAPTER FIFTEEN

CHAPTER ONE

"What do you mean you promised the matched ponies to Hannah Bontrager?" Eli Yoder said a little louder than he'd meant to.

He hadn't wanted to raise his voice with the matchmaker, but disappointment clouded his judgment and his ability to see reason.

"I'm sorry, Eli," Miss Sadie said. "I forgot that I sort of promised her a couple of years ago when I'd sold my other pair. She told me if my broodmare ever had another matched pair that she wanted them. She reminded me of it when she came to see me yesterday! I guess I forgot since she was only here visiting for the summer with Laney that year."

"We can't both have them!" Eli said, blowing out a discouraging breath. "I guess I'll have to settle for one of them, then."

Sadie Bieler shook her head slowly. "*Nee,* I'm afraid I can't do that; I can't break them up. I'd rather keep them myself than separate them."

Eli jutted out his chin and clenched his jaw as he did a little figuring in his head. He knew the matchmaker couldn't keep them easily herself because to her, and they'd be nothing more than hay burners. "I'll just have to offer you more, then." It would be a stretch, and it would take him longer to get a new buggy, but he'd have to make the sacrifice.

Again, the matchmaker shook her head slowly. "*Nee,* I can't do that either; I set my price—and it's a fair price, and I won't think of charging a cent more for them; that would be dishonest."

He threw his hands up and let them drop to his sides. "So that's it? Hannah gets them, and I don't have any say in it?"

"Let me think about it and see if I can come up with another solution," Miss Sadie said.

Eli could tell she felt terrible, but that didn't help his situation any.

"I'll think about it too," he said, even though from where he was standing, there was no solution that was going to be in his favor.

"Why don't you come by tomorrow afternoon and I'll have Hannah come too," she offered. "Perhaps if we put our heads together, we can come up with an answer that is fair to both of you."

Seth knew at this point the only fair thing to do was for each of them to take one pony, but he didn't like that idea; he wanted them both, and he was confident Hannah did too. With Miss Sadie refusing to break up the matched pair, one of them was going to be sorely disappointed, and he had a feeling it would end up being him.

"Why didn't you tell me Hannah was there to see the matched ponies when I talked to you yesterday?" Eli barked at his cousin.

Seth shrugged. "I didn't think it was that big of a deal."

Eli yanked off his straw hat and tossed it up in the air. "It *is* a big deal; the matchmaker promised them to both of us! She won't let me pay more than her price because she said that wouldn't be right, so she said we might have to compromise; you know Hannah's father will do everything he can to make sure she gets those ponies because she's spoiled!" He raked a hand through his dark blonde hair and bent down to pick up his hat where it landed in the grass.

"I wouldn't worry about it," Seth said. "The matchmaker is a fair woman, and she'll figure something out if she said she would."

Eli blew out a breath. "I suppose you're right, but she shouldn't have promised them to both of us in the first place."

"Did she say why she did that?"

Eli pushed his hat back on his head. "*Jah,* she said she promised her a few years ago and forgot all about it."

"You believe her, don't you?" Seth asked.

"*Ach,* of course, I do, but that doesn't make it any easier," Eli said with a sigh.

"When were you supposed to pick them up?"

Eli frowned. "They'll be two years old next Friday; I've only got until then to convince Hannah of how much I want those ponies!"

"That's only a week away," Seth said. "How are you going to get her to change her mind?"

"I don't know, but I'll think of something," Eli grumbled.

Seth chuckled. "You can always marry Hannah; then they'd be half yours!"

"That's not funny!" Eli said with a scowl. "I wouldn't marry that spoiled woman if she was the last woman in the community! I'd rather give up the ponies."

"You might have to change your mind about that, Cousin," Seth said.

Eli shook his head angrily. "It's not Friday yet; I'll think of something that won't involve having to fight that woman for them— or marry her!"

****

"What am I going to do, Laney?" Hannah was practically in tears. "Your boyfriend's cousin is trying to take my matched ponies from me!"

"I thought you liked Eli," Laney said.

"I never said I liked him, and I like him even less now that he's trying to take my matched ponies from me!" Hannah complained.

"They aren't yours yet!" Laney said.

Hannah folded her arms across her front and huffed. "Don't remind me!"

"What do you think the matchmaker is going to do about it?"

"I just came from there visiting with the ponies, and she said to come back tomorrow and meet with her and Eli," Hannah said. "She's going to try to come up with a solution, and she wants me to think about it too."

"Why don't you just take one of them and let the other one go to Eli?" Laney suggested. "That seems like the fairest solution."

"I half-heartedly suggested that to her, and she said Eli already asked and she said she doesn't want to break up the pair. I don't want to have to give them up to Eli; I don't even want to have to give one of them up to him. He'll make them plow horses, and I want them for riding. They're too pretty to be workhorses, and besides, they already know me and come to me when I visit them."

"What if he wants them for riding too?"

Hannah shook her head. *"Nee,* that's not practical for him; he's a farmer, and he would make them work in some way. I don't even want to use mine for pulling the buggy."

Laney smirked at her. "They can be buggy trained and still be *gut* for riding. Or you can use one for pulling your small buggy and the other for riding; you don't need two riding horses. I could train them for you and see which one works better for each."

"I don't think it's going to matter," she cried. "That awful Eli is going to take them away from me!"

Laney pulled loaves of piping hot bread from the oven and set them on the counter to cool. "Why don't you wait to get yourself all upset until after you meet with them tomorrow. If you don't get the solution you want, then you can get all worked up. I think you're worrying for nothing."

"I don't want to meet with them!" Hannah said, slumping down into the kitchen chair.

"Then you might have to share them with him."

Hannah sat up straight in a huff. "Share them? How do you suppose I'm going to share them unless Miss Sadie keeps them? Besides, that would mean I'd have to spend a lot of time around Eli, and I'm waiting for the matchmaker to find me my perfect match. I can't have Eli hanging around when I'm trying to court someone; I don't think another *mann* would put up with me spending time with another while I'm courting him."

"Then court Eli," Laney said.

Hannah sucked in her breath. "I won't court him; he's trying to take away my ponies!"

"If you married him, then you could both have them."

Hannah pursed her lips. "I'm not going to marry a *mann* just so I can have a matched pair of ponies the matchmaker already promised me. I'm certain Miss Sadie wants to meet with us both so she can let Eli down easy."

"What if she doesn't?" Laney asked. "What if she lets you down easy instead?"

Anger filled Hannah and tears threatened; her breath heaved, and she had to pull in a couple of deep breaths to calm down. She wasn't about to cry in front of her cousin; the woman would not understand her desire to have the ponies. She was too practical of a woman and would say they were a waste unless they were earning their keep. Her cousin didn't care that Hannah wanted to ride them, and there was no amount of talk about how unpractical it was for a working farm to keep two hay burners just for the sake of riding that would change her mind.

Laney turned around and glared at her cousin. "I thought you came over here to help me by making supper so I could finish sewing my wedding dress."

Hannah rose from the chair with a huff. "Go finish your dress; I'll finish making supper."

Hannah waited for her cousin to leave the room before she let the tears of worry fill her eyes. She bit them back just as quickly when a plan to outsmart Eli sprang to her mind. Maybe if she made Eli think she was interested in him, she could persuade him to change his mind and let her have them. She had a week to work her whiles on him since the ponies would have their birthday next Friday and wouldn't be able to leave the matchmaker's farm until then.

Would she be able to convince Eli in one week that they could be together as a couple, or would he reject the idea and see right through her?

Hannah washed up several potatoes and began to peel them as she thought of every possible way she could get those ponies away from Eli, and wooing him seemed to be the best way.

CHAPTER TWO

Hannah finished ironing her best blue dress; it was only for Sunday church services, but today was a special day, and she wanted to look her best. If she could get Eli to see her as a marriage prospect, he would let his guard down long enough to let her get the ponies away from him.

Laney would surely scold her for coming up with such a scheme, but she was the one who gave her the idea in the first place; so what if she would only be pretending to like Eli as a means to get the ponies for herself. She couldn't bear to see the beautiful creatures used as plow horses, and that's exactly what Eli would do with them.

Hannah tied her organdy apron and smoothed back her auburn hair, placing the matching organdy prayer *kapp* above the bun tied at the nape of her neck. Showing some of her hair was something the women did when they were courting; it was a means of flirtation, and she meant it that way today. Staring at herself in the mirror, Hannah couldn't help thinking she looked like a bride. The very thought of it put butterflies in her stomach, and she had to remind herself she was only pretending. If she was to get the ponies, she had to keep her head about her and keep her heart out of the mix; if she let her guard down, he'd get to her, and he'd get the ponies. She couldn't have that. Besides, Hannah saw him as nothing other than a good-looking shallow man who was full of himself. She wanted a man with substance; his good looks would fade in time, and she'd quickly become bored with his self-centered attitude. The matchmaker promised her a perfect match, and she would wait for that; in the meantime, she would have a little fun with Eli and get the ponies out from under him so quickly, he'd wonder how she managed it.

Hannah giggled to herself as she checked herself in the mirror one last time; if this didn't do it, then she would believe Eli to be a blind fool.

****

Eli put on his best blue shirt, his Sunday broadfall pants, and his good suspenders. He combed back his hair and topped off his look with his best black hat and polished his shoes. He wanted to look his best just in case he had to resort to his *plan B* to get those ponies away from the spoiled Hannah. Seth had given him the idea of marrying her, but he didn't want to; pretending he was interested in her would work, wouldn't it?

He gave his shoes an extra polish and then checked himself in the bathroom mirror. He smiled at his reflection, thinking Hannah was going to find him so irresistible she'd be begging him to take the ponies instead of her, thinking she would have partial ownership as soon as they married. The only catch was; Eli had no intention of marrying the spoiled woman, and nothing was going to change his mind.

****

Hannah arrived at the matchmaker's house just behind Eli; when he hopped out, her heart did a somersault, and her cheeks turned hot thinking about how handsome he looked.

Focus! She reprimanded herself. *I'm here to get those ponies, not to admire Eli in his Sunday best; I'll make him admire me instead.*

Hannah flashed him a flirtatious smile as he walked over to her buggy and extended his hand to help her down.

"*Danki,*" she said with an added measure of sweetness when she took his hand. She hadn't expected the warmth from his skin to send little prickles of excitement up her arm, and she giggled nervously without meaning to.

"I'm so glad to be able to meet with you and Miss Sadie today," she said, hoping to recover from her mistake.

He smiled as he let go of her hand and offered his arm to her for the walk up the porch steps.

Why is he being so helpful to me? she asked herself. Was he up to something? Perhaps he thought that being kind to her would make her want to give him the ponies.

Not a chance!

She looped her arm in his and let him walk her to the porch and up the stairs, the heat from him radiating through his long-sleeved shirt. Miss Sadie was waiting for them on the porch with refreshments, and Hannah felt her heart beating at breakneck speed. She was either about to get both ponies, or she was going to lose them both, and she almost feared both outcomes but didn't understand why.

****

Eli felt the warmth from Hannah's arm through the sleeve of his shirt, and it gave him the same tingly feeling as when he'd touched her hand, helping her down from her buggy. Her beauty had all but taken his breath away when he'd first laid eyes on her—as if seeing her for the first time. If he didn't keep his focus on the reason he was here—to get the ponies, he was going to lose this battle for sure and for certain. He assisted her up the stairs where the matchmaker was already waiting for them; it made his heart speed up to think he could be just minutes away from getting both horses to himself or losing both to this spoiled woman who had obviously put on her Sunday best to distract him. Even her smile told him he was in for a fight; it was sweet and welcoming, and almost made him want to kiss her, but he supposed that was the point. Had she thought to try to distract him the same way he had the intention of doing with her? Surely, she didn't think he was dumb enough to fall for such a scheme—especially when he'd thought of it first!

****

"Yesterday, both of you suggested breaking up the pair, and now you're both telling me you don't want to do that?" the matchmaker asked.

Eli and Hannah looked at each other and then shook their heads.

"Would you like me to decide which of you gets both ponies?" she asked with caution.

Again, they looked to each other, and then both nodded.

Sadie blew out a breath; they were not going to make this easy on her.

"I suppose the only way is for you each to guess the number I have in my head," she said.

"Seven!" Eli and Hannah shouted at the same time.

"I said it first!" Hannah squealed.

"I think I said it first!" Eli argued.

Sadie furrowed her brow; these two were going to give her trouble all the way till next week if she'd let them get away with it.

"I heard you both at the same time, and it was the right number so that won't work," Sadie said with a sigh. "I think the only way to decide this fairly is for the two of you to decide."

"Nee, that wouldn't be fair!" Hannah squealed. "He isn't going to let me have them."

"Are you going to let *me* have them?" Eli asked her.

"Nee, but only because you wouldn't let me have them either."

Sadie held up a hand to stop the next argument; it was apparent they could keep this up all day, and she had other appointments. It would seem that the only way to get them to agree on anything was to throw them together and make them both work for the ponies.

"I think the only way to decide this dilemma is to have a contest," she said.

"What kind of contest?" Hannah asked.

"What do you suggest?" she asked Hannah.

She was almost afraid to suggest it knowing it would likely cause another argument, but perhaps it was the best way to throw them together. After all, it was the lesson they needed to learn, not the competition itself.

"How about a cake baking contest?" Hannah said with a smirk.

Judging by the furrow in Eli's brow, Sadie would have to say she was right about this causing an argument too.

"You know full well I can't bake a cake!" Eli barked.

Hannah stuck her nose in the air and smiled. "I didn't know any such thing; plenty of *menner* in the community can bake cakes."

Eli scoffed. *"Jah,* if they're widowers!"

"I can't help it if you can't bake a cake," she retorted.

"Why don't we have a hay-baling contest?" Eli suggested. "We'll see how many bales of hay you can stack in five minutes."

Hannah sucked in her breath. "That wouldn't be fair!" she squealed. "Look at your muscles; I don't have muscles like that."

Eli flexed his arms and smiled, and Hannah huffed and folded her arms.

"Miss Sadie, you have to decide," Hannah begged.

With a deep breath, Sadie braced herself for a new argument. "If I decide, will the two of you abide by my wishes?"

Eli and Hannah eyed one another and then gave curt nods; she could tell neither of them wanted to agree but feared they had no choice. As far as she was concerned, they didn't because she wasn't going to give them one.

"It's my decision that if the two of you are going to compete for the chance to buy the matched pair of ponies, you'll have to submit to *both* contests."

"What?" they both said with raised voices.

Sadie put up a hand to stop them from going any further with their objections. "You will have to both bake a cake here at my *haus,* so I can be the judge, and you can bale the hay at the Bishop's *haus* since I happen to know they just did a haymow out at his place and he was waiting for the outer layer of the bales to dry before putting them in his barn. They should be ready for pickup in a day or two, is that right?" She turned to Eli for the answer to that one.

****

Eli sat opposite Hannah, and he wished he'd have sat next to her where he wouldn't be able to be distracted by her. Sitting here, it was tough not to be distracted by the warm summer breeze that played with the strings of her prayer *kapp* and a few strands of loose curls that had fallen from the clump of hair at the base of her neck. He knew from talking to Seth that a woman lets her hair fall out of the bun if she's trying to flirt with a man. She continuously tucked it behind her ear, but the wind would push it back across her face; she smiled at him, and it caused him to gulp his lemonade. He nearly spilled it down the front of his shirt but caught it in a big gulp he feared would surely bring an equally sized burp from his throat. He put his fist in front of his mouth, anticipating it, but it luckily didn't rear up.

He pulled his gaze away from the lovely Hannah; what was the matchmaker saying? Had he missed something?

He cleared his throat. "What did you say?"

"I asked if the bales of hay would be ready to load in a couple of days?" Sadie repeated.

"What hay bales?" he asked.

"At the Bishop's *haus*," she said. "Haven't you been listening?"

He gulped not wanting to admit he was distracted by Hannah. "*Jah,* I heard you, but it didn't register, that's all."

He could feel his cheeks heating, and Hannah let out a giggle; he cast his eyes down, knowing she'd just managed to get one up on him, and he didn't like that. If he didn't start paying attention, he was going to lose this fight altogether, and that's just what the spoiled Hannah wanted.

CHAPTER THREE

Hannah stopped rocking in the wicker chair on the matchmaker's porch and furrowed her brow.

"Wait a minute!" she said. "If we do both contests then I'm going to win the baking contest, and Eli is probably going to win the hay-baling contest, so how will that help us?"

"Probably?" he asked.

"There's a chance I could win that," she said with a smirk just to make him think she was confident.

"Not a chance at all, you mean!"

"We'll see!" she said, smiling.

He folded his arms across his chest and looked away from her. Finally, she was getting under his skin; if that didn't work, she'd have to resort to flirting with him again, and she didn't want to do that.

"Let's not put the buggy before the horse," the matchmaker said. "I agree that it's possible we would be at a draw when the contests are finished, but if that's the case, we might have to have a tie-breaker of some sort, but let's cross that bridge when we come to it."

Eli agreed, and so she did too, not wanting to appear uncooperative. If she gave the matchmaker a hard time about this, the woman would be reluctant to work with her to find her a match for marriage.

"This is your last chance to agree to splitting them up or for one of you to bow out and let the other one have both ponies," Miss Sadie said. "Otherwise, do we have a deal, then?"

Hannah glared at Eli as if to send him a silent message that he better not change his mind. She didn't want the pair separated, and unless he was going to bow out, which she doubted, she wanted him to be silent. She was never going to relent and give the ponies to him, so she nodded her head to the matchmaker's question. He nodded after, and Hannah flashed him a pleasant smile for cooperating.

"If there is no more arguing, then both of you can be here tomorrow after dinner; we'll do the baking then," the matchmaker said. "You can bring whatever ingredients you need, but no recipes will be allowed."

"I can't do that!" Eli argued. "I need a recipe for the cake to turn out even halfway right; I can't bake, remember?"

"Then I suggest you learn!" Hannah said with a giggle.

****

Eli went over to see his mother after leaving the matchmaker's house feeling more discouraged than ever, but if anyone could help him win that contest, his mother could. If he could win the cake baking contest, then he'd get those ponies for sure and for certain. There was no way Hannah could beat him at baling hay; the only advantage she had was baking a perfect cake. He'd tasted her cakes at the meals after the Sunday service, and they were as perfect as she was beautiful. The only other person he knew that baked a better cake was his own mother. Maybe he was a little bias because she was his mother, but both his mother's cakes and Hannah's were so close to perfection, it might be tough for the matchmaker to make up her mind. If he won the cake baking or it was a draw, then he'd still be a shoo-in for the win because unless Hannah gained ten pounds of muscle overnight, there was no way she was going to beat him at that event.

He knocked on the door to his mother's new home which she now shared with his uncle; it was still strange to him that the two of them married, but he was getting used to it. When she answered, she greeted him with a warm smile and a hug.

"Why are you so dressed up? Did you go to see the Bishop?"

"Nee, the matchmaker!"

His mother's eyebrows raised, and a smile crossed her lips. "You're getting a match?"

"Nee, I'm trying to get her matched pair of ponies."

His mother nodded, and her smile faded. "I hear Hiram Yoder is buying those for his *dochder,* Hannah."

Eli scowled. "Not if I can help it."

"How will you stop him?" she asked. "He is the wealthiest in the community, and Hannah is his only *kinner."*

"Ach, the matchmaker says because we both want them and she doesn't want to decide which one of us gets them, she decided we would have a contest to see who *wins* the right to purchase them."

"That sounds fair."

Eli shook his head and blew out a loud breath. *"Nee,* it's not; we are competing on which of us can bake the best cake and I can't bake."

His mother shooed him with her hand and smirked. "I will give you my best recipe, and you will win!"

Eli cast his eyes to the floor of his mother's kitchen noting she'd brought her hand-woven wool rug with her and it was now in her new home.

"We aren't allowed to use a recipe; we have to bake it from scratch and from memory."

"Are you allowed to bring all the ingredients?" his mother asked.

His gaze lifted, and his heart beat an extra thump from excitement. "*Jah,* that means I can bring the exact measurements of all the ingredients and all I have to do is memorize the order they go in and the temperature and time to bake it for. I'm a shoo-in for the win!"

"Do you think that's cheating?" his mother asked.

"I don't see how," he answered. "She didn't set down, but one rule and that was *no recipe* allowed, not even to be used as a reference. I thought that gave Hannah an unfair advantage, but if I can bring everything prepared and ready to go, the rest is a *cakewalk!"* he said with a chuckle.

His mother frowned. "I hope you're not setting yourself up for a fall."

"What could possibly go wrong?" he asked. "Hannah doesn't stand a chance against your salted caramel drizzle cake that everyone in the entire community can't get enough of."

His mother went to her recipe box which she now kept on her new counter and sifted through the box until she came to the recipe he wanted. "Copy it on another sheet of paper so you can get the ingredients from the store and then you can use that to memorize how to make it."

She hugged Eli when he finished copying down the recipe. "I wish you luck and a win if that's what will make you truly happy."

He gave his mother a quick squeeze. "*Danki, Mamm,* this win will make me the happiest *mann* in the community."

"I hope you're right," she said.

He dashed out of the house and hopped into his buggy and headed for town to the local grocery store. He had the recipe for the win and all the confidence in the world now. Not only was he going to win both contests, but he was also going to get those ponies away from the very spoiled Hannah.

****

Hannah knew Eli was going to run to his mother and get her salted caramel drizzle cake recipe, and if he could pull it off and manage to make it as well as his mother, he'd win with it. What could she do? She had nothing to compete with that cake; his mother usually had to bake five of them for everyone to get a tiny sliver of it on Sunday when they shared the meal. Everyone rushed to the line to get a piece before it was all gone; she, herself, had tasted it many times and thought it to be the most delectable dessert she'd ever tasted, and the women in the community were known for their baking skills. That cake by far would win if she didn't do something to stop him. Could she bake that cake? She'd tasted it enough times to figure out the ingredients, hadn't she? If she could duplicate the recipe, she could surely bake it better than the muscle-bound man who would be clumsy in the kitchen and nervous about winning. That alone would give her the advantage, wouldn't it?

She sat at the kitchen table and began to write down the ingredients that she could remember when her father entered in from outside.

"Is there any *kaffi?* " he asked as he removed his muddy boots at the door.

Hannah rose from the chair and poured him a fresh cup of coffee and set it on the table across from her.

Her father sat down and sipped his coffee and smiled. "What are you working on there?" he asked, pointing to the recipe.

"I'm trying to remember what is in that caramel cake the widower—I mean, the new *frau* Yoder makes for Sunday service," she said. "I thought I might make one."

"Why don't you wait until Sunday; I'm sure she's baking a batch of them to bring."

"I can't wait until then," she said with a squeal. "I have to win the contest tomorrow."

"What contest?"

"The matchmaker won't sell me the ponies because she promised them to Eli Yoder *after* she promised them to me, so now she's making us have a contest to win the right to buy them from her."

Her father set down his cup and leaned back in his chair. "Well, that hardly seems fair when she promised them to you a couple of years ago. Do you want me to go over there and talk to her?"

Hannah felt her heart thump. "*Nee,* then I will be teased as a *boppli* who has to have her *vadder* fight her battles for her. I'd rather do the contest and see how it works out. If I don't win, then you can talk to her."

"If all you have to do is bake a cake you should be able to beat that young *mann.*"

"*Nee,* he's going to use his *mudder's* caramel cake recipe, and that will win over any cake I can bake."

He nodded. "I see your point; you can ask your *mudder* when she gets back from her *brudder's haus,* but *frau* Yoder might have given her that recipe."

Hannah jumped up and looked in her mother's drawer, where she kept her recipes; she hadn't thought of that possibility. She raked through the drawer of loose pages, and hand-written recipes that contained stains and some had yellowed with age until she finally came across a relatively new one. She read the top line and let out a squeal.

"This is it! *Danki, Dat!* Now I can make the same cake and win the ponies!"

"Does this mean I don't have to pay for them if you win them?"

She giggled. *"Nee,* it means I get to buy them instead of Eli."

"Are you sure you want to compete with him with his own *mudder's* recipe?"

Hannah smirked. "Of course I do; it's the only way I'm going to have an advantage over him in this contest because I won't be able to win the other contest."

"What's the other contest?"

"We have to lift bales of hay onto a flatbed wagon and whoever can throw the most bales up in five minutes wins!"

Her father chuckled. "How do you think you're going to win that?"

"I'm probably not, but if I win the cake baking and he wins the hay baling, then we will be at a tie, and she will give us a tie-breaker," Hannah said.

"What about getting just *one* of the ponies," her father suggested.

"Nee!" she squealed. "I don't want just one; I want them both."

Her father let out a sigh, and she didn't like it when he did that; it usually meant she was in for a lecture.

"I know you have your heart set on that matched pair of ponies, but do you think it's wise to go up against Eli Yoder?"

"Why shouldn't I? What's the big deal if I go up against him or any other *mann?* It's to get those ponies."

38

"You will get yourself a certain *reputation* for being unruly, and since you're of marrying age and I happen to know you have your heart set on getting the matchmaker to find you a match, she might have a difficult time getting the young *menner* in the community to court a woman who is so competitive. *Menner* want a woman who is quiet and reserved and who will serve her husband—not be the one to wear the pants!"

"I don't want to wear the pants, *Dat,*" she tried to assure him. "But I don't want to stand aside and let a *mann* take away my ponies; don't you think I should fight for them?"

"If you win the ponies, you might lose something more important," he warned her.

Hannah bit her bottom lip as she stared at the recipe that would win her the ponies. Was her father right about the win coming at a price higher than she wanted to pay?

CHAPTER FOUR

Hannah gathered her bags of ingredients for her cake from the back of her buggy.

"Let me help you with that," Eli said from behind her.

She turned around, noting he was wearing a smug grin and it irritated her; it was apparent to her that he intended to make his mother's cake and was overconfident he was going to win with it. Luckily for her, she'd ignored her father's advice and intended to win with that very same recipe.

"*Danki,*" she said with an equally confident smile.

They walked side-by-side up to the porch of the matchmaker's house, Eli's arms loaded down with bags. Miss Sadie met them on the porch and welcomed them inside. Eli set the bags down on the counter, and Hannah pushed hers aside from his.

"Are you two ready for the contest?"

"I'm ready!" Eli said.

His confidence made Hannah cringe just a little, but she tried not to let it show. Instead, she ignored him and began to get her ingredients from her bag and take them to the kitchen table. Eli did the same as if he was keeping an eye on her. When she finished, she looked at his ingredients, which had been individually packaged in plastic bags.

"Hey, that's not fair!" she squealed. "He premeasured all of his ingredients so he wouldn't have to make it from memory."

The matchmaker sighed. "I didn't make a rule against it, so he's not disqualified; I'm sorry, Hannah, but the contest goes on unless either of you wants to bow out and forfeit to the other one."

"I'm not giving up!" Hannah said.

"Me neither!" Eli said.

Hannah pursed her lips determined not to let him get to her; if she lost her concentration, it would be all over for her.

"You may begin any time," the matchmaker said. "Just promise me you'll both keep a civil tongue in your heads."

Hannah nodded and then Eli agreed.

Getting out her large mixing bowl from her bag, Hannah began to mix the sugar and butter and then cracked four large eggs into the container.

Eli did the same, but she ignored him because most cakes started out the same. She hoped it would take him a few minutes to catch on that she was making the same cake—or maybe she'd get lucky, and he wouldn't notice at all.

Eli whipped his cake batter around the bowl until he saw how Hannah was stirring hers and began to mimic the way she was doing everything, but she continued to ignore him. She greased and floured her round cake pans, and he did the same.

Once the cakes were in the oven, she asked Miss Sadie for a small iron skillet to caramelize her sugar, and Eli asked for the same thing. They stood side-by-side at the stove, caramelizing their sugar, and then set it aside. Then they both mixed heavy cream, vanilla, and butter and brought it to a boil on the stove and then mixed it in with the caramelized sugar. Separating about a cup aside, they mixed in powdered sugar in with the rest of it to make a creamy icing.

Eli looked over at Hannah finally and blew out a long breath. "Why are you copying everything I do?" he barked.

"I'm not copying you; I'm making the same cake, silly *mann!"* she said with a giggle that irritated him.

"Ach, how did you get the recipe for this cake? It was *mei mudders* secret cake."

"It's not such a secret because she gave the recipe to *mei mudder* and now I'm going to win with your *mudder's* cake recipe!"

"That's not fair!" he grumbled.

"All's fair in pony war!" she said with a snicker.

"How is either of us supposed to win with the same recipe?" he asked.

"That's not my problem!" she said curtly.

By the time the cakes were cooled, neither of them had spoken for more than fifteen minutes. They'd cleaned the kitchen and all the utensils in silence while Miss Sadie sat quietly in the other room in her rocking chair crocheting a blanket.

Hannah began to spread the top layer of her cake with the frosting while Eli did the same to his. Once both layers were slathered in frosting, they both drizzled the caramel over the top and then sprinkled coarse sea salt and pecans on top. Looking between the cakes, Hannah couldn't really tell the difference except that they were on two different colored cake plates. She let out a sigh and glanced over at Eli, who was also busy studying the two for any differences.

He shrugged. "Now what?"

Hannah called for the matchmaker to join them in the kitchen, and she entered the room with a satisfying smile when she spotted both cakes on the table.

The matchmaker looked between them for several minutes before speaking.

"It looks to me like it might be a tie," she said.

"But you didn't even taste them!" Hannah complained.

She smiled. "I don't have to; I'll let the two of you decide who the winner is!"

"But…" Hannah started to argue.

"The milk is in the refrigerator," Miss Sadie called over her shoulder. "Enjoy!"

Hannah stood there with her mouth hanging open for several minutes, and Eli didn't move.

"What do we do now?" Hannah asked.

Eli smiled. "I guess we eat!"

Hannah went to the cupboard and got two plates, cups, and found a couple of forks in a drawer and brought them to the table while Eli got the milk from the refrigerator.

Then Hannah sliced pieces of each cake and put one of each on their plates, setting one in front of Eli. After she poured the milk, she sat across from him, and he reached across the table for her hand and then bowed his head for a prayer. It struck her funny that he would pray over the cake unless he was afraid to eat it, but she placed her hand in his and bowed her head too. Warmth radiated from his hand to hers, and it gave her a strange feeling of comfort that she didn't want to end.

He lifted his head and slowly let his hand separate from hers; the warmth remained, and her fingers still tingled, but she didn't dare let him know how it had affected her.

Both sat there quietly for a moment, and Hannah waited for him to take the first bite. He turned his fork to the side and cut a large chunk of her cake first; she held her breath in wait for his reaction.

He closed his eyes as he chewed it slowly, the corners of his mouth curving up into a smile.

He nodded and opened his eyes, the smile remaining. "I think yours is really *gut.*"

"Really?"

He nodded and took another bite. "Really!"

Hannah took a bite of Eli's cake, and her eyes went wide with delight, her smile genuine. "This is tasty!"

Eli smiled and puffed out his chest. "You're surprised?"

"*Nee—jah*—well, a little, but it's so *gut!*"

"*Danki,*" he said with a chuckle.

They both took a bite of their own cake. "They're both perfect!" she said.

"*Jah,* I agree," Eli said. "They're both perfect; so now what?"

Hannah shrugged.

"I guess this means it's a draw," Eli said.

Hannah shook her head; she was not going to let this be a draw. She needed to win this round of competition in order to stay in the game.

"Let's have Miss Sadie try them to see if she can decide."

Eli shook his head. "*Nee;* she told us to decide. We both agreed that they are both perfect, so that makes it a draw."

"But…" she started to say.

"Don't argue with me, Hannah," he warned. "It's not an attractive trait for a *fraa.*"

She sucked in her breath. "I'm not your *fraa!*"

"*Nee,*" he agreed. "But you will be someone's *fraa* someday, and I'm telling you as a *friend* that *menner* don't want to be married to an argumentative woman."

Hannah clenched her jaw, embarrassment creeping up her neck and settling on her warm cheeks. her father had warned her of the same thing just yesterday, but she didn't care about Eli's opinion: his opinion didn't count. He'd called her a friend; did he mean it? She gazed into his warm blue eyes, thinking that maybe—just maybe, he did.

****

Eli hadn't meant to come off as being harsh with Hannah, but for some reason, he felt the need to reprimand her. She was acting like a spoiled child, and he didn't want her to think that kind of attitude would sit well with him or any other man. It was something he would tell his own sister if she was acting that way. So why did he care so much? Was it possible there was more to the attraction he felt for her?

He watched her eat the entire piece of the cake he made, and he loved how amazed she seemed at his baking skills. For this moment, Eli would put aside the matched pair of ponies; he simply couldn't get enough of her smiling blue eyes that seemed to melt his heart, and he intended to enjoy every minute of it that he could before reality ruined it for him. Was there more to his attraction for her? Was his reprimand of her for his benefit or for hers? One thing he knew for sure; he could admire her all day—especially while she was enjoying his cake—the cake that not only broke the barrier between the two of them but between him and the matched pair of ponies.

****

Sadie thought for sure she was going to have to break up a fight or two with that pair in her kitchen, but the passion between them seemed to be much stronger than their fight. She eavesdropped on their conversation, thinking they might need a nudge here and there, but once they started eating cake, the tension seemingly wore off, and they finally began to relax with each other. It did her heart good to know that test she was putting them through was breaking them of their pride and selfishness. So far, her plan was working, but if they managed to catch on to her scheme, it could backfire on her, and she'd have to resort to some tough love for the both of them. Before the week was over, they might need it, but for now, all was calm with a little bit of sugar to sweeten things up. Nothing made her happier than to see two young people discovering themselves and each other, and these two were going to learn a lot before she was finished grooming them for their perfect match.

CHAPTER FIVE

Hannah dropped all of her bags onto the table that weighed down one arm and then set the remainder of the cake she'd baked beside them. Before leaving the matchmaker's house, Eli had asked for an extra thick slice of her cake; had he thought hers was just a little better than hers and hadn't admitted to it? Not that it mattered; the matchmaker had declared this round of competition between them to be a tie.

"How did your day go?" her mother asked with a bright smile.

Hannah slumped into the nearest chair and rested her elbows on the table, cradling her chin in her hands. She sighed. "I'm not sure."

Her mother sat across from her and pushed aside the bags to get a better look at her daughter and then opened the lid on the cake box.

She clucked her tongue. "You used Eli's *familye* recipe for the contest?"

Hannah looked at her mother and resisted the urge to roll her eyes. "*Dat* already warned me not to, but I did it anyway."

"I'm guessing he made the same cake?"

Hannah lifted her head and nodded with downcast eyes.

"Did he win?"

She shook her head. "Miss Sadie said it was a tie before she even tasted them."

Her mother scoffed. "I would have done the same thing; I can see just by looking at this cake that it is exactly like the ones his *mudder* brings to the Sunday meals. I guess you two made a matched pair!"

"*Mamm,* that's not funny," Hannah grumbled.

"You are both very stubborn; it's a *gut* trait to have if the two of you were working together, but you were working against each other," her mother said. "If you could harness that stubborn quality and make it work for *gut* and not for bad, the two of you would make a nice matched pair."

"I don't want to be matched with him!" Hannah squealed.

"Why not? What's wrong with him?" her mother asked. "He's handsome and a hard-working farmer; he has his own home and land, and he would be a *gut* provider."

Hannah sighed. He was all of that, but she wanted more. "I don't want a *mann* who is *practical;* I want to be matched with the right one—the one who will make me fall in love with him."

"There aren't any *sparks* between you and Eli?"

Hannah didn't have to think about that one; there had been some sparks, but she didn't fall in love with him over it. Her cousin, Laney, had told her when she was in love with a man it would hit her like a strong wind that put butterflies in her stomach and a smile on her face that would never fade. A few sparks were not enough to convince Hannah that she should consider Eli for a match.

"He's too competitive!"

"I happen to know that you are also competitive," her mother said.

"Having that in common is not enough to build on for a solid marriage," Hannah said with a roll of her eyes.

"I agree, but it is a trait you can make work for you—if you work together the way I suggested."

"How can I work *with* him when we're fighting for the same thing?"

Her mother smiled. "I think you just fell into the answer to that question."

Hannah blew out a discouraging breath and let her head fall against her folded arms across the table. Her mother was a wise woman, and there had to be something to what she'd just said—but what? The only way she and Eli could both get the ponies was if they split them up and each took one or if they joined forces and shared them. She doubted her future husband would permit her to own a pair of matched ponies with another *mann,* so what was the solution? She wasn't about to marry him just to get ownership of the horses, especially when she'd likely be in a constant battle with Eli over the use of them. He was too practical of a man to let her keep the hay burners strictly for riding purposes.

"May I try a piece?" her mother asked.

"*Jah,* let me get you a plate," Hannah said, rising from her chair.

Hannah sliced off a piece of her cake and gave it to her mother. She took a bite and made a face, and Hannah felt her heart skip a beat.

"What's wrong?"

Her mother finished chewing and swallowed the bite of cake. "It's much saltier than the one Eli's mother makes; it's a *gut* cake, but I think you added too much salt to the frosting."

Hannah lifted the lid of the cake box and cut the thick slice of Eli's cake she'd brought home with her and plunked it on her mother's plate. "Try that one!"

Her mother bit into it and smiled as she chewed. "This piece is much better."

Hannah sucked in her breath. "That's Eli's cake!"

"What did the matchmaker say about the winner?"

Hannah sighed. "She didn't say anything; she let us decide, and we both agreed it was a tie."

"Eli said it was a tie?"

"*Jah,* he did."

"You both tasted each other's cakes?" her mother asked.

"*Jah* and we both agreed it was a tie," Hannah said. "I thought mine tasted a little saltier, but I didn't say anything to him at the time. Do you think he noticed it was too salty?"

Her mother smiled. "I'd be willing to bet he did."

"Then he made it a tie instead of winning and ending the competition right there; why do you suppose he did that?"

Her mother shrugged and smiled. "Only time will tell."

Hannah felt more confused than ever; was Eli up to something or had he really not noticed her cake was not as good as his? She tasted them both again. Hers was too salty; there was no denying it. He'd eaten his entire piece and asked for a thick slice to take home with him; had he merely humored her?

****

Eli put away his horse, wondering what had gotten into him at the matchmaker's house. His cake was clearly superior to Hannah's, but he'd been a coward not to tell her so. Instead, he'd declared that hers was just as perfect as his own had turned out. Perhaps he was being biased; did he dare ask his cousin for a second opinion on the cakes, or should he just let it go? He'd had the perfect chance to challenge the matchmaker to judge the cakes and give her opinion, but he'd let it go. Looking into Hannah's welcoming blue eyes had made him feel weak in the knees over her.

"Did your *mudder's* cake win?" Seth asked him as he entered the barn.

Eli shook his head. "I'm not really sure what happened there today; any chance you want to taste both cakes and tell me which one is better? I feel like I need a second opinion."

"You won me over at the mention of cake!" Seth said.

"I brought a piece of hers and have mine too, but I don't want you to know which is which, so go sit at the table under the oak tree in the yard and I'll bring the plates out to you."

Eli closed his horse in the corral and went toward the house.

"Don't forget the milk!" Seth hollered after him with a chuckle.

Eli went in and brought out the two pieces of cake and a glass of milk on one of his mother's trays she'd left behind after moving out. He set them in front of Seth and let him test it. He'd put each slice on two different plates so he would be able to tell them apart. Sitting across from his cousin, he waited for Seth to taste a few bites, but the anticipation was driving him mad.

After several bites, Seth put down his fork and looked up at his cousin. "This one on the yellow plate is just a little bit better than the one on the white plate; I think you added to much salt to yours."

"That's what I thought," Eli said. "That one is too salty; only, that one isn't mine. It's Hannah's."

"It's a real *gut* cake if you don't get too much of the icing, but the salt on the icing is what gives it a bad taste. What did the matchmaker say? I guess you won since your cake is better."

"She didn't taste them," Eli said. "She made me and Hannah decide."

"So you won, then," Seth said. "Congratulations!"

Eli shook his head. "When the matchmaker came in and looked at the cakes, she said it looked like we had a tie; honestly the cakes looked identical."

"But they don't taste identical, so your cake won."

"It's not that easy," Eli admitted.

"Why not?" Seth asked. "Go back to the matchmaker and ask her to taste them and declare you the winner; those matched ponies are all you've talked about since they were born. I know how much you want them— unless you've changed your mind."

"*Nee,* I haven't changed my mind, but I'm thinking there is a better way to get them besides hurting Hannah to get them."

Seth chuckled. "You've got it bad for her, don't you?"

Eli scoffed at him. *"Nee,* you're narrish."*

"Ach, the only reason a *mann* forfeits to a woman is if he wants to marry her!"

"I wouldn't go that far," Eli said. "But you didn't see the hope in her eyes; she wanted her cake to win so badly, I didn't have the heart to tell her it wasn't as *gut* as mine. You can't tell a woman her cake is not as *gut* as a cake baked by a *mann.* Women take pride in their cooking skills; it's what gives them the tools to be a *gut fraa.* I couldn't take that away from her, or she wouldn't have the confidence she needs to marry someday."

"Why do you care so much about how she feels about marrying?"

"I admit I was angry at first when I realized she made *mei mudder's* cake, but then I realized that was something she needed to win—as a woman."

"Just make sure I get an invitation," Seth said with a chuckle.

"To what?" Eli asked.

"To your wedding!"

"That's not funny; I didn't say I wanted to marry her. I just didn't want to shatter her confidence that she'll need to win herself a match."

"Keep telling yourself that, Cousin," Seth said, eating the rest of Eli's cake.

"Don't worry; I will."

Eli went into the house and took another bite of Hannah's cake with a big glop of frosting on it; he shuddered at the amount of salt in it, but he chewed it and swallowed it, just like he'd swallowed his victory today at the cake competition.

CHAPTER SIX

After the service, Miss Sadie pulled Eli aside to talk to him. "I tasted both the cakes yesterday; why didn't you ask me to taste them and make my decision in your favor before you left *mei haus?* You won the cake competition, so that puts you in the running."

"*Nee,* Hannah and I both agreed it was a tie," he answered.

"Didn't you taste that hers was too salty?" the matchmaker asked him. "In my opinion, that makes you the winner."

Eli lowered his head. "*Jah,* I tasted it, but I didn't have the heart to tell her, and I wish you wouldn't say anything either. She expects me to win the hay baling competition; I don't need to win both to make a point or get the ponies."

The matchmaker smiled. "I agree with you, and I believe that attitude shows real maturity. I have a lot of respect for you for not wanting to hurt Hannah."

"*Danki,* but I only did it because I felt it was the right thing to do."

The matchmaker pointed to Hannah sitting under a tree alone; she seemed to be sulking. "I think she could use a friend; her *mudder* told me this morning she knows her cake wasn't as *gut* as yours; perhaps the two of you should talk."

Eli nodded; the last thing he wanted was for her to feel bad. That's what he was trying to avoid by letting her think they were a tie for the cake baking yesterday. How had things gotten so complicated? He pulled in a deep breath and walked over to her, determined to fix what he'd broken.

When he approached, she looked up sadly, and it almost broke his heart.

"May I sit with you?"

"Did the matchmaker tell you that you had to sit with me?" she asked.

"*Nee,* I saw you over here alone and thought you might like some company."

"*Danki,*" she answered. "That would be nice."

He held his hand out to her. "Would you like to take a walk with me down by the lake?"

She took his hand, and he assisted her up from the ground, her warm hand sending tingles all the way up his arm. Was he falling for her the way his cousin accused him? He wouldn't say anything to her about the cake if she didn't bring it up; there was no point in making her upset. He preferred it when she smiled.

"Are you hungry?" he asked. "We can eat first if you'd like."

She shook her head. "I'm not really hungry; not yet. We can go for a walk first. I was happy to get out of the stuffy *haus*."

"*Jah,* it was hot in there today; the Bishop should have opened the windows to let in this nice breeze."

"He gets chilly," Hannah said.

"Well, he is getting on in years, so I suppose the rest of us have to accommodate him; after all, it is his *haus* that we had the service today."

"Maybe in the summer we should rotate around to other's homes so we can keep the windows open," Hannah suggested.

"Nee, I think he plans it that way all summer so he won't get too cold when he's conducting the service."

Hannah sighed. "I suppose you're right about that."

"Besides," Eli added. "It's nice to have the meal with the lake view, don't you agree?"

"*Jah,* he is lucky he lives on the lake."

Eli pulled in a deep breath and smiled. "It is mighty peaceful here."

When they reached the lake, Eli offered his hand to her so they could go across the dock. She placed her hand in his, and he felt that warmth again. He liked it, and he wondered if she felt it too, or if it was only him. They stopped at the end of the dock, and he began to pull his shoes and socks off.

"What are you doing?" she asked.

"I'm going to cool off," he said. "Would you like to join me?"

She giggled and began to pull off her shoes and long socks.

They sat down on the end of the dock and dangled their feet in the water; they were sitting so close their legs touched, and it warmed Eli up. Thankful for the cold water to keep him from sweating from the warmth of her touch, he swished his feet a little, kicking up a splash of water.

"Hey!" Hannah said, wiping her face. "You splashed me!"

"Oops; sorry."

She kicked her feet hard and brought lake water up on both of them. He blocked his face but couldn't help laughing at her efforts to get him soaked. She giggled and splashed with her feet, and he joined her, laughing just as hard as she was. By the time they finally stopped, his shirt and pants were just as soaked as her dark purple dress was, but somehow, her hair had managed to stay dry.

Eli removed his black hat and wiped his face. "I think we're going to have to stay down here until we dry off unless we want a scolding from the Bishop."

Hannah wrung out the skirt of her organdy apron and nodded. "I think you're right about that, but that sun is so hot today, we'll be dry in no time."

"You don't mind waiting that long to eat, do you?" he asked.

She giggled. "I'm afraid I'll have to since you soaked me to the skin."

Eli threw his head back and laughed. "Since I soaked you? You're the one who started splashing."

Hannah bit her bottom lip and flashed him a mischievous smile. "Well, you should know better!"

"I should know better?" he asked. He was laughing so hard he couldn't even keep a straight face and neither could she. "Well, if I don't know enough not to get myself soaked—and you too, then I don't know better than to keep from jumping in and taking you with me!"

Hannah squealed and tried to get to her feet, but he caught hold of her and wrapped his arms around her, acting as if he was going to jump off the end of the dock.

"Stop; stop!" she squealed with laughter.

He pulled her closer and looked into her eyes, the anticipation there between them. With his gaze locked onto her deep blue eyes, he bent toward her, his lips nearly touching hers. His breath heaved with anticipation as he waited for a signal that his advance would be welcome. The Bishop's voice behind them broke the spell, and they scrambled to separate from each other.

He called their names once more, and Eli's attention turned from Hannah to the other end of the dock where the Bishop stood with his arms folded, a stern look in his eyes. Eli reached behind his back for Hannah's hand, and she slipped her hand in his, remaining behind him.

"You stay here and let me handle this, understand?" he whispered over his shoulder to Hannah.

"Jah, okay," she said with a quiet, shaky voice.

He gave her shaking hand a squeeze and let go; he walked to the end of the dock, leaving Hannah behind. He walked with intent toward the Bishop; he would defend their actions to the man while protecting Hannah. There was no reason to involve her; he was the one who pulled her into his arms and tried to kiss her without thinking about how many members of the community were in the back yard of the Bishop's house overlooking his actions down here at the lake.

He stopped at the end of the dock in front of the man and clenched his jaw as he looked him straight in the eye. He would take the full brunt of the man's reprimand alone; today, he would be a man.

"It is my understanding you and Hannah will be picking up the bales of hay in my field on Wednesday, ain't it so?"

Eli let out the breath he'd been holding in; wasn't he going to get after him for their public display of affection?

He cleared his throat. *"Jah,* that is true."

The Bishop nodded and then let his gaze travel to Hannah at the end of the dock. "I was wondering if you would mind coming early and getting all the bales except the ones you intend on using for the competition."

Eli coughed and then cleared his throat again. *"Jah;* did you want both of us to show up early or just me?"

He flashed Eli a half-smile. "Just you."

Eli felt his heart beating faster than a runaway horse. He nodded. "I'll be there."

The Bishop nodded and then turned to leave but turned back. "Tell Hannah her *mudder* was looking for her."

Eli gulped down the lump in his throat. "I'll tell her, *danki.*"

He stood there for several minutes watching the Bishop walk slowly back up to the yard where the rest of the community seemed oblivious to their talk—if he could call it that. The Bishop had had a strange gleam in his eye—as if to relay an unspoken message that he too, was young once and he understood, but his coming down there was to act as a warning to be more careful in front of the watchful eyes of the community. Eli appreciated him not reprimanding him, especially in front of Hannah. They were grown and still in their *rumspringa* time, and though the community usually looked the other way when the youth got out of control during that time in their lives, there was an unspoken forbiddance of it.

Eli walked to the end of the dock and smiled at Hannah as he picked up her shoes and handed them to her. "He said your mudder is looking for you."

Her jaw went lax. "That's all he said?"

"He asked me to come early on Wednesday to bring in the entire crop of hay for him before the competition."

"You'll be exhausted by the time we have the competition," she said.

He winked at her. "Then I suppose you'll have an advantage over me."

She smiled. "I'm okay with that!"

He reached for her hand, and she offered it willingly. "After you see what your *mudder* wants, will you share the meal with me down here by the lake?"

"People will think we're courting," she said.

"I think they already do," Eli said with a smile.

Her eyes grew wide. "Do you think we're courting?"

Eli shrugged. "I don't know; maybe. I don't think I would have tried to kiss you a few minutes ago if I wasn't thinking about it."

She let her hand slip from his and flashed him a strange look. "I better go see what *mei mudder* wants."

"What about lunch together?" he asked as she was running down the dock, her bare feet slapping against the wooden slats.

She turned around when she reached the end of the dock and flashed him another strange look. "I'll let you know."

Eli picked up his shoes and sat on the end of the dock to put them on; had he spooked her with all that talk about courting? She'd been in tune with him and had even shared an intimate moment with him until the Bishop had interrupted them. He thought they'd made a real connection—up until he mentioned them courting. Would she have let him kiss her if they hadn't been disturbed? He'd been overcome with the desire to hold her and kiss her, and though she seemed to want it too, he had to wonder now if she'd been pretending—but why?

CHAPTER SEVEN

Hannah ran up the slope that led to the lake where she'd left Eli alone; she feared losing her head again the way she almost had when he'd tried to kiss her. Would she have let him if the Bishop hadn't stopped them from making such a huge mistake? But was it really a mistake? She could feel herself falling for him, but she worried it might be a trick to distract her from getting the ponies.

Lord, how will I know if I can trust him? Please show me a clear sign because I think I'm falling in love with him and I don't want him to break my heart over the ponies.

When she found her mother, she was out of breath and had to sit down.

"Why were you running, Hannah?" her mother asked. "Did the two of you have an argument? It looked to me like you were getting along fine, but then things changed."

Hannah fumed. Why did he have to try to kiss her out in plain view of the entire community? Now she would never get her perfect match from the matchmaker; everyone thinks she's courting Eli. If he's only using his charm to get her to give him the ponies, then she'll lose the ponies and her perfect match, and she will end up a lonely spinster. How could she have been so foolish as to fall for him?

"*Nee,* we didn't have an argument," she said. "The Bishop said you were looking for me."

"*Jah,* I was worried you would be hungry, and I didn't see you down there at first until Eli's *mudder* pointed the two of you out; she agreed you make a nice match."

Hannah sighed. "We're not a match, *Mamm,* and I'm not hungry."

"Go sit in the sun for a little while and dry off," her mother said, looking her up and down with a disapproving scowl. "I'll bring you something in a little while. Take my quilt so you'll have a comfortable place to sit in the grass."

Hannah took the quilt from her mother and walked away, her head hung low with embarrassment; on the way down to the lake—away from the dock where Eli still was, she kept her eyes cast down, avoiding eye contact with everyone she passed. Right now, she was in no mood to be around anyone, and she wished she'd have brought her own buggy so she could go home and go back to bed. Maybe if she slept, she'd be able to start the day over again. She slumped to the ground after spreading out the blanket and leaned back, allowing the sun to warm her damp dress. She felt torn between wishing she could take back the close encounter with Eli and wishing he'd have had the chance to kiss her so she would know for sure what her true feelings were for him; right now, she was so confused she couldn't think straight.

She raised her head and leaned back on her elbows, looking out at the ripples of sunshine gleaming off the lake's surface. It was too pretty of a day to sulk, but she didn't know how to change the way she felt. A slight breeze played with the bits of hair that had come loose from the back of her prayer *kapp*. It was wet, and she unpinned it and pulled down her damp hair, hoping it would dry in the gentle breeze. At this point, she didn't care who saw her with her hair down. She'd already pushed the boundaries with her public display down at the dock. She was sure to get a reprimand from her father later about her behavior, but she hoped she could get away with it by using the *rumspringa* excuse.

She blew out a long sigh and closed her eyes against the warm sun hitting her face.

"May I join you?" Eli asked from behind her.

She turned around, noting that he had two plates of food with him and a thermos tucked in the crook of his arm. Truth-be-told, she was starving and was happy to see the offer of the food at least.

She nodded, and he handed her one of the plates.

"I wasn't sure what you like best, so I brought you my favorites," he said with a smile.

She looked at the plate containing two fried chicken legs, potato salad, a corn muffin, and chow-chow. "*Danki,* they're my favorites too!"

He smiled as he sat next to her on the quilt and then pulled her hand into his and bowed his head for a prayer. "Lord, please bless this food before us and bless those who prepared it. Please forgive me for embarrassing Hannah and help her to forgive me for not showing her more respect than I did today. Bless our friendship, Amen."

"Amen," Hannah whispered.

He slowly pulled his hand from hers but not before he gave it a quick and gentle squeeze. Was it possible he really did care for her? Surely, he wouldn't lie in a prayer; she didn't take him to be that kind of man.

"I forgive you," she whispered.

He looked over at her and smiled, lifting a chicken leg from the plate. "Let's eat while the chicken is still hot."

She picked up her chicken and bit into it, unsure if her nervous stomach would allow her to eat everything on the plate. She was hungry indeed, but the butterflies disturbing her at the moment had her wondering if she was beginning to get that love feeling that her cousin had described to her.

They ate their meal in silence, but it was nice not to have to talk. Surely, now that he was sharing the meal with her, everyone would believe they were courting. Was she okay with that; was he? She had to find out.

"I suppose they will all believe we are courting now," she said quietly.

"Would that be so bad?" he asked.

She shrugged. "*Jah,* if it isn't true."

"If I asked you to court me, would you say yes?" he asked, his blue eyes gleaming in the sunlight.

"Are you asking?"

He smiled, and the butterflies churned around in her stomach, leaving her with a funny but pleasant feeling.

"*Jah,* I'm asking," he said.

This was her chance; if she could convince him she was interested, she might be able to get the ponies away from him. He'd already declared the cake baking competition a tie even though she was sure he knew her cake was not as good. If she played along, she would win, she was certain of it.

"Then I accept!" she said, pasting on a smile.

The butterflies did another turn in her stomach when he smiled again. Was her heart betraying her? If she really loved him and he was genuinely interested in her, she would lose him *and* the ponies if she wasn't careful. She let out a sigh thinking she would see how things played out. Thankfully, they had a few days before the next competition. Perhaps between now and then, he'd try to kiss her again, and she would know for sure. He wouldn't kiss her if he was faking a relationship with her, would he? No man would sink that low just to get a pair of matched ponies. At least she prayed he wouldn't.

Eli went back to eating, and though she was too nervous to eat, she forced herself to eat slowly, knowing the sudden silence between them was more welcome than if they tried to over-analyze it the way she was in her head.

"Would you like to attend the singing with me this evening?" he asked.

Her heart slammed against her ribcage. Going to a public event like that would be like an official announcement. Them sitting here now was not much better, but at least they wouldn't have to show up somewhere together. She'd be leaving the picnic with her mother, and he would be taking himself home.

"I'd like to take you home from the meal today too if that's alright," he said. "I guess that would sort of make things official between us, *Jah?"*

"Jah, it would," she agreed. "I don't really feel up to the singing tonight because I have to get up so early tomorrow for washday; I have to do extra because it's the beginning of the month and all the bedding has to be changed, and I have to wash the summer quilts." She had no idea why she was rambling on, except that she was nervous.

"I understand," he said. "I'll settle for driving you home this afternoon."

"Danki, I'd like that." Was that her own voice betraying her?

What was she going to do now? Laney was going to demand details from her, and she had no idea what was going on; everything was happening so fast. She felt dizzy and confused; did she like him enough to dive in with both feet right now, or was she digging a big hole she would fall into later?

When they finished eating, he asked if they wanted some dessert. She nodded, thinking that even if she couldn't eat it all, it would give her time to think while he was away, and when he returned, she would have something to occupy her shaky hands.

When he returned, he had slices of his mother's salted caramel drizzle cake. Did he have to bring that?

She smiled and took a bite; it was heavenly.

"This is so much better than the cake I made yesterday," Eli said.

Hannah swallowed the bite of cake. "I have to admit that it's ten times better than mine too." She looked into his kind, blue eyes and couldn't keep the truth from him any longer. "If I'm being honest; yours was even better than mine."

He chuckled. *"Nee,* it was a tie, but I will agree that *mei mudder's* cake is better."

Had he really not tasted the difference between their cakes, or was he falling for her and didn't want to cause her heartache by telling her the truth about her awful cake?

****

86

Eli was so happy that Hannah admitted his cake was not as good as his, that he was almost beside himself; to him, he was sure that meant she really cared about him and wasn't just humoring him to get the horses. Maybe Seth was right, and the only way for them both to be happy about the matched pair of ponies was to get married and share them; now that they were courting, it was something to consider. But right now, he was happy she cared about him, and that made his need for those horses somehow not as important.

When they finished their cake, he helped them slip away from the crowd gathered around the lake. After finding her mother, they let her know they were leaving, and she seemed pleased. She'd pulled them both into a hug and promised to keep their news between them for now—no sense in alerting the entire community to their personal business.

Eli helped Hannah into the buggy, wondering if he was going to feel that exciting, electric surge every time they touched. He climbed in beside her and put his arm around her once they exited the Bishop's driveway.

She didn't pull away from him; instead, she moved in a little closer and put her head on his shoulder. Was this what love felt like? If so, he didn't care about those ponies at all; he'd be content spending the rest of his life with Hannah in his arms. He chuckled inwardly thinking she was the last person he thought he'd want to spend his life with, but life could sure put an unexpected fork into the road every once in a while.

CHAPTER EIGHT

Hannah allowed Eli to hold her hand as they walked along the edge of the lake. It was strangely exciting taking a buggy ride with him; he'd taken his time taking her home from church yesterday, but this was their first official buggy ride.

"How long will you and your *familye* stay in the community?" he asked.

"*Dat* is making plans to buy the *haus* we're renting," she answered. "We started renting the *haus* so that we could be near since Laney's *mamm* died, but my parents want to stay. They said it's too much work to keep moving back and forth—especially when we don't have any more *familye* back home."

"I'm so happy to hear you'll be staying."

Hannah thought he sounded relieved they wouldn't be leaving. Did that mean he was anticipating a future with her?

"I'm happy about it too," she said with a smile.

He swung their arms gently as they walked, their fingers entwined. A slight breeze from off the water made her shiver.

"Are you cold?" he asked.

It was a damp night, and the dew had collected on her feet that were clad only in a pair of flip flops. She hadn't thought even to bring a sweater.

"Maybe a little," she said.

Was that the wind that was putting butterflies in her stomach, or was it Eli, who suddenly stopped in front of her and was slowly pulling her into his arms.

"Let me warm you up for a minute," he said with his gentle baritone.

She leaned into him, those butterflies working overtime. He bent his face into her neck, and it sent shivers all the way to her toes. When his lips began to sweep over her neck and up her chin, her heart began to beat wildly; it almost made her dizzy. The cricket's song faded, and the frogs chirping became muffled; all she could hear was the frantic beating of her own heart. Her breaths were like a panting dog as he whispered in her ear.

"I love you, Hannah," he said softly, sending tingles from her ear to her toes.

"I love you too!" she whispered back breathlessly.

His mouth finally found hers, and she swooned. His arms were strong around her, and she deepened the kiss as her fingers raked through his thick hair.

Had he said he loved her? Had she said it back to him?

Her heart raced, and she kissed him with wild abandon; she loved him, and he loved her, and she didn't care who knew about it.

****

Hannah ran up to her room from the back steps, so she didn't have to give her parents an explanation of her whereabouts for the past few hours; she was late getting home and didn't want to have to account for the time. Eli had just dropped her off so she was sure they'd heard his buggy, but she was too giddy to talk to either of them right now. If she did, she feared she would give away all her feelings about him, and she wanted to keep that to herself for now. She prayed her mother wouldn't come upstairs and pry about her evening with Eli.

They'd spent most of the time riding around and talking, but then they'd gone to the far side of the lake opposite the Bishop's house and sat on the dock some more. There was one thing that bothered her though; he hadn't brought up the matched pair of ponies once the entire day. Had he forgotten about them the way she had until the ride home? They'd had such a wonderful time talking that they'd lost track of time. He'd expressed some concern about the fact that her family had only been in the community for the past year after the death of her aunt. Once she'd reassured him that they were staying, he seemed a lot more relaxed.

It wasn't until he kissed her that she realized he must be in love with her.

Hannah lit the lamp on her dresser beside the door; she jumped when something moved on the other side of the room and turned up the wick so she could see. Her hand flew to her chest when Laney sat up in her bed and stretched.

"I must have fallen asleep reading my book waiting for you to get home," Laney said, stretching again.

"You nearly made me wet my pants!" Hannah said.

"What time is it anyway?"

It was after midnight, but Hannah didn't want to admit it. "It's not that late," she answered.

"Your buggy ride must have gone well," Laney said, waggling her eyebrows.

Hannah crossed the room and pretended to search for her pajamas. "That's none of your business,"

Laney sat on the edge of the bed and smirked. "He must have kissed you!"

Hannah could feel her cheeks warming; she couldn't admit to that, could she? Her silence and red cheeks were surely giving her away.

She nodded slowly; truth be told, she was bursting to tell someone. She and Laney had never been close, and it was mostly her fault. This was her chance to change that with her cousin.

"*Jah,* he kissed me," she gushed. "It was just the way you told me it would be; I felt the butterflies rushing over me like a strong, cool breeze that left me with shivers, and I can't stop smiling!"

Laney rose from the bed and rushed to Hannah's side, surprising her by pulling her into a hug; it was nice—almost like having a sister to confide in.

"Are you staying over tonight?" Hannah asked her.

"*Jah,* if that's okay."

"I'm not going to make you go home this late," Hannah said. "Besides, I need someone to talk to; I need some advice."

Laney smirked. "You want *my* advice?"

"Don't be so surprised."

Laney sat down on the bed and patted the spot beside her. "Sit; let's talk. I'm awake now, and I'm too excited for you to go back to sleep just yet."

"Don't be too excited for me," Hannah warned her.

"Why not? You just told me you were in love and he kissed you! The two of you didn't have a fight already, did you?"

"*Nee,* nothing like that, but he covered up the fact that my cake was awful for that baking competition. I knew it was bad, and I didn't say anything, but I brought it up tonight, and he said it wasn't true; he said we had a tie and that just wasn't true. Why would he do that?"

"Maybe he really does love you, and you shouldn't question it; just go with it and be happy," Laney suggested. "I see that as unconditional love; when a *mann* will eat a woman's cooking no matter how bad it is and say it's better than anything he's ever tasted, that *mann* can't sense anything else except the love in his heart for you."

"But if you look at it from a different angle," Hannah said. "If he would have given me the win for the cake competition knowing he is going to win the hay baling competition, then the matchmaker would give us a tie-breaker—hopefully, something we would each be able to compete reasonably without one having an advantage over the other the way these competitions were. At least that way I'd have a fighting chance."

Laney shook her head. "The way I see it, he had the advantage over you in both categories, so making this one a tie since there was no way the matchmaker would accept you as the winner when his cake was clearly superior to yours, he is giving you a leg up. Isn't he supposed to go and load up the entire field *before* the competition day after tomorrow?"

"*Jah,* what does that have to do with anything?" Hannah asked.

"He's going to be wiped out, dragging himself, exhausted by the time you arrive for the competition and that gives you a full advantage over the hay baling. So if you can manage to load more bales of hay on the wagon before he can then you win the entire thing!"

"I see your point!" Hannah said, giggling.

"Do you think it'll cause problems in your love life if you win the ponies?

"Why should it?" Hannah asked. "He asked if he could court me; if we end up married, the ponies will belong to both of us."

Laney nodded.

Hannah sucked in her breath suddenly. "You don't think that's the reason he asked to court me, do you? Because he knew he had a chance of losing, and if we get married, we both win?"

Laney shook her head. "A person wouldn't court someone just to get their hands on a set of matched ponies; no one would sink that low, would they?"

Hannah gulped; a couple of days ago, she'd been guilty of considering that very thing.

****

"You're home late!" Seth said.

Eli chuckled. "You weren't waiting up for me, were you?"

"*Nee,*" Seth said with a smile. "I was over at my place building cabinets trying to finish the inside until I couldn't keep my eyes open any longer."

Eli pointed to the cup of coffee between his cousin's hands. "So you decided to come back here and have *kaffi* so you could get to sleep easier?"

Seth smirked. "I'll admit I figured I'd sit here for a few minutes and wait to see how things went; judging from the hour, I'd have to say it went better than you expected, *Jah?*"

"Jah. I told her I loved her."

Seth sat a little straighter in his chair, his full attention on his cousin. "What did she say?"

"She said she loved me too."

"Do you believe her?"

Eli smiled. "She kissed me as if she loves me; why wouldn't I believe her?"

"You don't waste any time, Cousin, do you?" Seth asked.

"She admitted she knew that my cake was better and should have won the competition; she wouldn't do that unless she really cared about me."

"I hope you're right, Eli; I don't want to see you end up with a broken heart when the week is over."

"If it's about the ponies," Eli said. "As far as I'm concerned; she can have them."

"Wait a minute, now," Seth warned him. "You don't want to give those ponies up; not when that's all you've talked my ear off about ever since you decided to buy them!"

"I just don't think they're worth losing Hannah over," Eli admitted. "I can always find another matched pair of ponies; I can't find another Hannah."

Seth shook his head and blew out a long breath. "I sure hope you know what you're doing, Cousin."

Eli nodded and smiled. "I do; I love her, and I'm willing to give them up to her if it means proving how much I love her."

"Why would you have to prove it to her?"

"Because she's been handed everything from her father all her life; I think she associates love with being given things."

"So how would you giving her the ponies prove that to her? Isn't that the same thing her father has done to confuse her all these years?"

"*Nee,*" Eli said. "His giving has always come easy for him; my giving is a great sacrifice, and I pray she'll see that. If she does, she'll know how much I love her because of what I'm giving up for her."

"I'm sure her father loves her too!" Seth said.

"Of course he does, but this is different; trust me, I know what I'm doing."

Seth shook his head. "I hope you're right about this and you don't end up holding your broken heart in your hands at the end of the week."

"If I don't do this to show her the difference now, then when we are married, she'll always expect me to make things easy for her the way her father has all her life, and I don't want to end up catering to a spoiled *fraa* all my life; it'll break my back."

Seth nodded. "I see your point."

"I pray she does too before it's too late," Eli said. "For both our sake."

Eli left his cousin in the kitchen while he dragged his tired frame off to bed; it had been a long and exciting couple of days, but the week ahead of him was going to drag on before they came to Friday—the day he would either get it all or nothing.

CHAPTER NINE

Hannah lifted the large rock and carried it over to the garden area where she let it drop with the rest of them; she was exhausted and collapsed to the soft ground beside the tomato bed.

"I've been watching you for the last few minutes trying to figure out what in the world you're doing!"

Hannah's breath hitched as she turned around to greet Eli. "Where did you come from?" she asked, catching her breath.

"I drove up a few minutes ago; you must not have seen me," he said. "I'm sorry; I didn't mean to startle you."

"I nearly jumped out of my skin!"

He held out a hand to help her up from the ground; she held out her hands and looked at the dirt smudging them and the lines of muck under her fingernails.

"Are you sure you want to touch me? I'm filthy!"

He held up his hands. "I'm not much better; I had to stop and fix the wheel on my buggy on the way here; I still have a little bit of axle grease on me; most of it wiped off though."

"Well, in that case," she said, extending her hand to his.

He helped her up and looked at the rock border she was making around the garden. "What exactly are you doing?"

She didn't want to admit she was trying to build her muscles for the competition tomorrow. "I'm making a border with the rocks *mei dat* dug from the field; I've been saying I was going to get to it for weeks, but something else always seems to take priority. Now that he's buying the *haus,* I figure it's as *gut* a time as any to get things done around here."

He chuckled. "You should save your strength for the hay baling tomorrow."

Having him remind her about the competition didn't sit well with her for some reason, but she shrugged it off.

"I would be happy to help you if you'd like me to," he offered.

"Shouldn't you be saving your strength too? You have to load the whole field for the Bishop."

"It's a small field," Eli said. "Don't worry about me; I'm more worried about you. Some of these rocks must have weighed a ton!"

Hannah looked at the little bit of progress she'd made in the last couple of hours. "Not quite, but close. I'm ready to take a break; can you stay for some lemonade?"

"I was hoping you'd offer me something," he said, removing his straw hat and wiping his sweaty brow with a handkerchief. "It's a hot one today, *jah?*"

"Jah," she said, lifting her black apron to dust off her hands. "I'll go in and wash up and bring us some lemonade out to the garden; is that alright?"

He nodded and flashed her a smile that made her weak in the knees. She went inside and washed, taking her time to fix her disheveled hair. Then she put together the lemonade tray and some sugar cookies for them. By the time she got back out there, Eli had finished one entire side of the garden, lining it with the decorative stones.

Hannah set the tray down on the table on the patio and rushed to the edge of the garden where Eli was still working. "You don't need to do that!" she squealed. "I can finish it later or next week."

"Nonsense!" Eli said. "This is *mann's* work; it's much too hard for you. You are going to be so sore tomorrow you won't be able to move."

Hannah rolled her shoulders. "I'm pretty sore now!"

"Then let me finish it for you," he said.

"I can't sit by while you do this for me; I'm sure you have chores of your own to finish."

"I do, but I don't mind helping you," he said, continuing to arrange the rocks.

"What you've done so far looks nice, *danki,"* Hannah said. "You can go inside and wash up if you'd like and I'll pour us some lemonade."

He looked up at her from where he was crouched on his haunches in her garden and flashed her a smile. "If you insist; but we can talk about it some more over the lemonade."

Her heart fluttered as she watched him go inside; he was the type of man who would pamper her and care for her if she married him. She could see that in him already; was that the kind of man she wanted? She giggled inwardly; she didn't have to give that much thought. Of course, she wanted a man who would dote on her; what woman wouldn't?

Truthfully, she almost felt as if she was taking advantage of his good nature, though.

She set up the refreshments and then sat on one side of the table, grateful for the large oak tree giving off shade for them. Waiting for him before she took a drink, her heart skipped a beat when he came out of the house, his hat off and his hair wet and slicked back. Oh, how handsome he was; it made the butterflies in her stomach twist and turn.

He sat next to her and pulled his chair closer, so their knees touched. "I missed you since last night," he said with a smile.

She giggled shyly, and he pulled his clean hands into hers. "I was on my way home, but I wanted to see you today; I won't be able to take a buggy ride tonight since I have to be at the Bishop's *haus* at first light. I'm going to have to be up at about three o'clock in the morning just to get my own chores done before I eat and head over there. I'm sorry about that, but I need to get a few hours of sleep."

"I understand; I'd like to get some sleep tonight too," she said. "We got in pretty late last night."

"I had a nice time with you," he said.

His words lingered thick in the air, and she could tell he had something else on his mind. "About the ponies; why do you want them so badly?"

There it was; he was going to try to talk her out of getting them by attempting to prove he needed them or wanted them more than she did. Well, she wasn't going to let him get away with making those ponies into workhorses if she could help it.

"Eli Yoder," she said, bouncing up from her chair. "I want those ponies for riding. I don't want to see them end up on the front end of farm equipment or pulling a buggy. Those ponies are too fine of animals not to be treated more like a pet than a practical addition to your farm equipment!"

"I agree with you about that," he said gently.

She sat back in her chair slowly, her jaw slack. "You do?"

"I'm not planning on using them to haul or to pull the buggy," Eli said. "I want to ride them. I feel the same way you do about them; they're beautiful animals. I know they aren't practical, and they'd be nothing more than pretty to look at and hay burners, but I think they should graze freely and occasionally be ridden, not worked to the bone."

Hannah felt her heart thump out of normal rhythm; it was apparent to her that he wanted those ponies for the same reasons she did which would make the loss just as heartbreaking for him as it would be for her. How could they settle this so both of them would be happy when the matchmaker refused to split up the pair? Would he share them with her if he won? More importantly, would she be willing to share with him if she was the winner? Sadly, she didn't know the answers to any of those questions plaguing her mind.

"I'm glad to hear that about them."

"Me too," he said. "It'll make me feel better about it if I don't win the competition."

Hannah swallowed the lump in her throat; the final competition was tomorrow, and she was sure she was going to lose. Eli was much stronger than she was, and she didn't stand a chance against him. Knowing herself and how she felt about them, losing the ponies would be a bitter pill to swallow. She gazed mournfully into Eli's kind blue eyes fearing she was about to lose him too. Whatever the outcome tomorrow, neither of them would ever be the same.

****

"What's wrong?" her mother asked.

Hannah bit back the tears that threatened to spill down her cheeks. "I can't go to the competition with Eli tomorrow; if I do, I'll lose. And if I lose the ponies, I'll lose him! I don't know what to do."

"What makes you think you'll lose him?"

"Because I'll be angry with him for winning."

Her mother opened her arms, and Hannah collapsed into them and began to sob. "I know you have your heart set on getting those ponies, but you can't have everything. Don't tell your *vadder* I said that because he thinks you should have everything you want, but real life doesn't always work out that way. He's spoiled you, and I never thought it was such a *gut* way to raise you. Now that you're a grown woman, I can tell you that. Sometimes, you need to experience what happens when you don't get your own way. I hate to say this to you, but losing those ponies might be *gut* for you; it will teach you more about life than having everything handed to you. If you're meant to have them and it's *Gott's* will, then you'll have them. But I think you should prepare yourself for a loss tomorrow—of the ponies and not of Eli. Isn't your future with the *mann* you love more important than those ponies?"

"Of course it is, but why can't I have both?"

"Perhaps if you trust Eli, then you will be able to have everything, but if you don't trust him, then you might lose the ponies and him too."

"I can't take that chance, *Mamm,*" Hannah sobbed. "I need to make sure those ponies are mine so I can have it all. I have to win tomorrow; I don't know how, but I have to."

"I'm afraid if you don't trust Eli any more than that," her mother said. "I'm afraid I have no advice for you. I think you should bow out of the contest and let him get the ponies. If he really loves you, then you will have them when he marries you."

"And what if he doesn't? Then I will lose it all."

Her mother lifted her chin to make her look her in the eye. "Then it is not meant to be, and it was not yours to begin with. If you have that little trust for Eli, then show up tomorrow."

"I've thought about not going, but I'm too big of a coward," Hannah admitted.

"Why do you suppose that is?"

"Because I already choked when we had the baking competition, and I lost; I don't want to lose this one."

Her mother smiled sadly. "Do you really think you stand a chance against Eli?"

She shook her head. "I already know that I don't."

"Then why bother to show up?" her mother said. "If you know you're going to lose the competition, stay home and then you will find out if you will get Eli *and* the ponies. You want to marry him, *Jah?*"

"Jah," Hannah said. "I love him."

"Then that is your answer; stay home."

Hannah knew that what her mother said was right, but she just wasn't sure if she could do that.

CHAPTER TEN

Hannah drove her buggy up to the Bishop's barn and got out, adjusting her work apron; she'd dressed for the competition just in case Eli didn't want to call it off. She'd had a restless night mulling over her mother's words and had made the decision to bow out and let the situation take care of itself however it would.

"I'm so glad you showed up," a familiar snippy voice came from behind her.

Hannah turned around and forced a welcoming smile for Cassie, the Bishop's youngest daughter. Though they were the same age, they'd never been friends; the lovely young woman always needed to be the center of attention with all the young men in the community and it got on Hannah's nerves. The girl was never without an audience for her dramatic stories where all the young men hung on her every word, hoping for a little bit of attention from her. Most of the young women saw her as a threat, but Hannah didn't pay her any mind.

"Hello, Cassie, how are you this hot summer day?" Hannah asked, trying her best to be polite.

"I've had a wonderful morning watching Eli Yoder in our field," she said. "And he was so happy to see me when I took some refreshments out to him a few minutes ago. But as I was saying; I'm glad you showed up. Eli is so tired out I'm sure you'll win this competition; then he can get rid of the silly notion of spending so much money on those ponies so they can sit around our barn and eat hay all day."

"*Our* barn?" Hannah asked. "You mean, *his barn?*"

Cassie giggled. "*Nee, our* barn," she said. "When we get married, I don't want those hay burners in the barn spending all of our money we will need for long winters."

Hannah's heart slammed against her ribs. "You are marrying Eli?" she heard her voice squeak out. "Did he ask you?"

"Not yet!" she said. "But when he drove me home last night, he was about to kiss me until *mei dat* interrupted him by coming out of the *haus.*"

Hannah couldn't think straight; Eli had come over to her house yesterday and told her he couldn't take her for a buggy ride because he had to get to bed early.

"He drove you home? From where?"

"The matchmaker's *haus,*" Cassie said with a giggle.

What a fool she'd been to believe that man and what he said. He didn't love her; he was playing her for a fool to get the ponies away from her.

She bit her bottom lip to keep the tears from giving away her emotions.

"Will you excuse me, Cassie; I have a competition I have to win!"

"I can help you if you'd like me to!" she called after Hannah. "Since there aren't any rules against it."

Hannah turned on her heels and faced Cassie, who wore a satisfied grin on her face. Though it made her angry, she would accept her help if it meant getting the ponies away from that two-timing Eli.

She nodded curtly. "*Danki,* I'll accept your help."

Cassie squealed with delight and skipped toward her. "Let's go win you those ponies!"

Hannah gritted her teeth and bit back the tears; who needed Eli? She would have her ponies in two days, and with Cassie's help, this competition was going to get her the win.

****

Eli looked up at Hannah and smiled as she approached the field where he'd spent the morning loading hay bales. He didn't like the look in her eye; it was competitive and stern.

"I'm here, and I'm ready to win those ponies!" she said to the matchmaker. "I have Cassie to help me; you said no rules, right?"

The matchmaker nodded at both of them and flashed Eli a pitiful look. He knew how tired he was; with Cassie's help, she would undoubtedly win. He'd never seen the two of them acting as friends before, but right now, they seemed closer than sisters. Cassie hadn't said anything to him last night about helping Hannah, but here she was, and it confused him.

"Are you up to the competition?" Hannah asked him; her tone was almost snippy.

"I'm up for it," he answered. He couldn't figure out what had gotten into her, but he suspected she and Cassie had talked and Hannah probably knew he'd given her a ride home last night. She seemed almost jealous, and he didn't take Hannah for the jealous type.

Well, if a competition was what she wanted, then he was going to give it to her—tired or not.

"Let's get this over with," he said, wiping his brow. He was tired and in no mood to compete with an unruly woman.

The Bishop held up his hand and waited for his pocket watch to give him the signal. "Go!" he said finally.

Cassie and Hannah each picked up an end of a bale and tossed it up onto the flatbed wagon before Eli could even bend down to pick up his first bale. His back was sore, and his shoulders were even worse, but he was going to give it his best.

Eli tossed his first bale, and the women were on their second bale. He threw a second one, and his shoulder nearly gave out. He took his time to get to the next bale while he listened to Cassie and Hannah scrambling behind him. They were grunting and groaning but cheered when they'd had another victory. By his count, that was three for Hannah, and he was still only on his second one. He was too tired for this, and he just wanted to go home and take a shower. He was soaked with sweat from head to toe, and every muscle ached from overwork in the hot sun. He felt weak and tired—almost faint as he bent to pick up his third bale.

Eli bent down on one knee and struggled to pick up another bale; he heaved it up to his shoulder and pushed himself to get it over to the flatbed wagon. He pivoted and let it drop; it caused the horses to shift and squeal. He went over to them and patted their necks and rubbed their ears for a minute.

"Sorry, fellas," he said, gently petting them to calm them.

"Time!" the Bishop called.

Eli turned around slowly and counted the bales at the back of the flatbed; Hannah and Cassie had managed to get six bales onto the bed, while he'd barely managed his fourth.

She won, and she was making no secret of it. She bounced on her heels, her smile wider than he'd ever seen.

"I won!" she squealed. "I won! Thank you, Cassie, for helping me win!"

Cassie smiled a devious smile that didn't go unnoticed by Eli. "You're so welcome; I'm so happy for you that you won!"

What was she up to?

His gaze fell on Hannah, who was all smiles; he'd never seen her look happier—except when he'd kissed her the other night. She was so beautiful then, but right now, his opinion of her had somehow darkened with her attitude about this competition. Nonetheless, she'd won fair and square, and he wouldn't begrudge her the win.

"Congratulations!" Eli said.

She flashed him a brief but curt smile and then went back to bouncing around and begging the matchmaker to let her go see her new ponies. It was enough to make Eli sick—but not to his stomach—his heart felt as if it was breaking in two. He hopped up onto the flatbed and pushed the team of horses away from the scene; he still had to unload the hay bales into the barn and then come back and pick up the last few in the field; he could have gotten them now, but he didn't want to be around Hannah right now and listen to another minute of her gloating over her win. It made him sad to think that they didn't even have so much as a friendship right now.

****

Hannah watched Eli drive away in the flatbed wagon, and it gave her a funny, sinking feeling in her gut. Gone were the butterflies she had for him, and in their place, bile rose to her throat. She swallowed hard against the pain and the burning of her hollow victory. Granted, she was excited at first, but when she realized what it had cost her, she suddenly felt ill. She watched Cassie chase after him, and it sickened her even more; at the very least, she and Eli were friends, weren't they? Perhaps there was nothing left to salvage with him— not even friendship. Cassie had made it clear she was going to marry him; if they had an appointment with the matchmaker last night the way Cassie indicated they did, then there was no hope for Hannah no matter what.

"I'll be over later," Hannah said to the matchmaker. "I have to go home and tell *mei dat* so he can come by and pay you for the ponies. *Danki,* Bishop Troyer for letting us have the competition here. Tell Cassie I said goodbye."

"Congratulations!" the Bishop said to her.

She nodded and said her goodbyes to him and the matchmaker and then went toward the driveway to leave. When she neared the barn, she could hear Cassie giggling and Eli saying something in a low voice to her. Not wanting to listen to what they were talking about, or to see either of them, she hopped up into her buggy and slapped at the reins to move her horse out of the driveway as fast as she could. She didn't want to be around to see the two love-birds celebrating.

As she went down the road a ways, she got to thinking that something just wasn't right about the whole situation; Eli had told her how much those ponies meant to him. Had Cassie somehow changed his mind, or was his meeting with the Bishop this morning what had done it? Was it possible the Bishop had put pressure on him to marry Cassie? She was the last of his seven daughters to get married, and the Bishop had made it no secret that he was anxious to have her married this wedding season. Was that the reason the Bishop had called him over to work his hayfield today?

Eli's feelings for her had seemed so genuine two days ago at the lake and then the night of their buggy ride. He'd kissed her like a man in love; he'd even told her he loved her. So what had changed? When he'd come to her yesterday in the garden, he was genuine, but he seemed distracted as if he had something weighing on his mind. Had he tried to tell her then that the Bishop was making him marry Cassie? Did he know then? Was he being forced into it, or was he marrying her willingly?

Hannah drove up into her yard and parked the buggy up near the barn. Her father came out and smiled. "Will you please take care of my horse, *Dat?* I don't feel so *gut;* I need to lie down for a while," she said with a shaky voice.

"How did the competition go?" he called after her.

Hannah didn't answer; she was too afraid if she turned around to face her father, she would burst into tears.

CHAPTER ELEVEN

Hannah ran past her mother and up to her room and threw herself onto her bed in a heap of sobs.

A knock at her door startled her; she bolted upright on her bed and wiped her face and sniffled. "Come in," she said with a shaky voice.

Her mother opened the door slowly and looked at her daughter with a sad smile. "I'm so sorry you didn't win the ponies, Hannah."

"But I did win!" she sobbed.

Her mother rushed to her bedside and sat next to her; she pulled her into her arms and smoothed her hair. "If you won, then why are you crying, Hannah?"

"Because I lost Eli," she sobbed, burying her face in her mother's shoulder.

Her mother clucked her tongue. "I warned you not to go and compete with him; I wish you would have listened to me."

"I did go there to tell the matchmaker I wasn't going to compete for the ponies, but when Cassie told me that Eli almost kissed her last night when he brought her home after their meeting with the matchmaker, I lost my head. She told me that they were going to get married, and it made me furious. So, I competed—with Cassie's help, and I won. I won the ponies away from him, and I'm glad! Except that now I'm miserable."

"You sound confused," her mother said. "I find it hard to believe that Eli is going to marry Cassie; he wouldn't do that after he told you that he loved you."

"I think the Bishop put pressure on him," Hannah cried. "He was trying to tell me something yesterday when he came over to see me—or maybe he was trying *not* to tell me something, but that was it. He knew yesterday that he was marrying Cassie and he didn't bother to warn me before I showed up at the Bishop's *haus* today."

"That doesn't make any sense," her mother said, soothing her. "Maybe you should talk to him and find out for sure before you make yourself sick with all this worrying and crying."

"I don't want to talk to him," she cried. "I just want to bury my head in my pillow and sleep until Saturday. I don't even want to go get the ponies now!"

"I was afraid this was going to happen when you told me you were competing with Eli over those ponies," her mother said. "I still think you should talk to the matchmaker at least about this. Maybe she can help you sort it out."

"I don't want to talk to her or anyone right now," Hannah cried. "I'm sorry, *Mamm,* but I don't even want to talk to you. I just want to be alone and think about all of this."

"I think that would be wise," her mother said. "But after you think about it, you need to talk to Eli to clear up the misunderstanding."

"It's not a misunderstanding, *Mamm;* he's marrying Cassie!"

"I don't believe that even for a minute, and I'm certain that once you calm down and give it some serious thought, you'll realize it too."

"*Nee,* I have to face the truth; he's marrying Cassie. She told me herself, *Mamm.*"

"*Ach,* you know as well as anyone in the community that the Bishop has his hands full with his youngest *dochder.* I'm not sure I'd take her word for it; it's possible she might have misunderstood the way I think you've misunderstood the way things are. The only way you'll know for sure is to talk to Eli himself."

"He's the *last* person I want to talk to right now!" Hannah squealed.

Her mother rose from the bed and folded her arms. "You think about it—pray about it. *Gott* will give you your answer even if the humans involved won't or won't be truthful about it."

She agreed to pray about it, and her mother finally left her to sulk alone.

****

Eli was worn out and too tired to deal with having Cassie on his heels. All he wanted to do was finish the job the Bishop had requested of him and go back home so he could think things through. He couldn't think straight with the chatty young woman getting in his way, but he couldn't be short with her. He would have a conversation with her later just as the Bishop had asked him to, but he wasn't up for it right now.

Thankfully, her mother called her inside the house to help make the afternoon meal, and Eli felt relief wash over him. He intended to finish the chore for the Bishop and get away before an invite to join them for the meal was extended to him.

Cassie turned around before she entered the house and waved to him. "Don't leave before we eat," she called out to him. *"Dat* wants you to stay and eat with us. Then we can go for a buggy ride."

Eli nodded and forced a smile; he was too tired and dirty to take a meal with the Bishop and his family, and too tired to take Cassie for a buggy ride the way she was expecting. He hoped it wouldn't come to that, but he had little control over the situation right now, and that irritated him.

"Tell him I'll be ready in about half an hour," Eli said, out of breath.

She giggled like a schoolgirl, and it grated on his nerves; there was no way out now. He had to do what the Bishop asked, and he was going to have to take care of it dirty and sweaty and tired. He groaned inwardly; how had he gotten himself mixed up in the middle of this mess anyway? It wasn't fair; it wasn't what he wanted to do, but it was the only way to keep peace with the Bishop.

****

Hannah stirred when someone knocked on her bedroom door; had she fallen asleep? The late afternoon sun streamed in through her window, making her squint. Another knock caused her to rise slowly from the bed and stumble to the door.

"What happened to you today?" Laney asked. "You were supposed to come over and tell me what happened with the competition."

"Nothing happened," Hannah said groggily and collapsed back onto her bed, burying her face in her pillow.

"Are you sick or something?" Laney asked, nudging her. "Your *mamm* said you'd been up here in bed all afternoon."

"She should have told you to leave me alone," she said, her voice muffled by the pillow.

"I guess you lost the ponies," Laney said. "I'm sorry."

Hannah lifted her head from the pillow and sniffled. "I didn't lose; I won!"

Laney gave her an excited jiggle. "You won? Then why are you up here crying like a spoiled sport?"

"Because Eli is marrying Cassie Troyer!"

"*Ach,* I guess that explains why I just passed the two of them on the road in his buggy."

Hannah buried her face deeper into her pillow and bawled like a cow who was having a hard time calving. Laney patted her back and shushed her.

"I'm sorry," she said. "I shouldn't have told you."

Hannah sat up and wiped her face. *"Nee,* I need the truth; it would have been nice to get the truth from Eli. I think he tried to tell me yesterday afternoon but chickened out like a coward."

"I'm so sorry about Eli," Laney said. "I never thought he'd turn out to be that kind of *mann."*

"Jah, I didn't either," Hannah cried. "I believed him when he told me he loved me. I believed it when he kissed me."

"I know it's no consolation, but at least you got the ponies."

Hannah glared at her cousin. "You're right; it's no consolation. What am I going to do?"

"You're going to enjoy your win and enjoy those ponies when you get them on Friday, and then you're going to get the matchmaker to set you up with a better match than Eli Yoder."

"But I love him!" Hannah sobbed. "How can I stop loving him so this will stop hurting so much?"

"I don't know," Laney admitted. "I think it's something that has to take time to heal—like when I lost *mei mamm.* Time heals all wounds—trust me."

"I don't want to be matched up with anyone else; I don't know if I'll ever get over Eli."

Laney smoothed back Hannah's hair that was damp from crying so much. "You will, but it will take some time."

"Until that time, I'm not leaving this room," Hannah said.

"Why would you let him steal your joy like that?" Laney retorted. "Talk to the matchmaker; she'll find you someone who's honest and better-suited for you. Let Cassie have him if he's going to be that kind of *mann!*"

"*Ach,* I know what you're saying seems right, but something is very wrong with this picture. I refuse to believe Eli would do that to me; he was so honest and genuine with me."

"What do you mean?" Laney asked.

"Something was bothering him yesterday when he came to see me."

Laney rolled her eyes. "His conscience, maybe?"

"*Nee,* I don't think that's it; he was almost upset. He started to talk to me about the ponies. I think he was going to ask me to bow out of the competition or maybe he wanted me to bow out voluntarily. Maybe he was testing me, and I failed."

"The only one who failed here is Eli; don't you dare blame yourself for his actions. Maybe the Bishop needs to straighten him out before he marries Cassie or the two of them will have a terrible marriage."

Hannah began to sob all over again at the thought of Eli marrying Cassie. She couldn't stay here and watch the two of them get married and have *kinner.*

"I'm going to ask *Dat* if we can move back to Ohio. I don't want to stick around here and watch the two of them living a happy life when I'm miserable."

"I understand," Laney said. "But we've grown pretty close since I got engaged to Seth and I'm going to miss you if you leave."

Hannah sniffled. "I'm going to miss you too; it's been almost like having a *schweschder.*"

"Jah, who will stand up for me at my wedding? I don't have anyone else I'd rather stand up with me than you."

"I'm sorry," Hannah cried. "I will try to come back for your wedding—if I'm feeling better by then."

"I wish you'd stay here; I don't want you to go."

Hannah stiffened her upper lip. "I have to go; if I don't, I'm afraid I'll make an even bigger fool of myself than I already have with Eli."

"What about the ponies? What are you going to do about them if you leave?"

Hannah shrugged. "The matchmaker told me she has another buyer who will take them if Eli doesn't want them, but I know his future *fraa* doesn't want them. She told me so herself. She said she didn't want those hay burners in her barn; she said they had more practical things to spend their money on—like having lots of *kinner."*

Hannah buried her head in her pillow and sobbed. She couldn't bear to think about

Eli having a family with Cassie. He would have a house full of kinner with her flaming red hair and his blue eyes, and she didn't want to stick around to see it.

"She actually said all that to you?" Laney asked. "She was certainly trying really hard to hurt you."

"Well, it worked; I'm so crushed I don't think I'll ever recover. And I'm not leaving this room until the house is packed up and we leave this community. Being here a year has been a year too long."

"I'm so sorry he broke your heart, and I'm sorry you have to give up the ponies. Are you going to tell the matchmaker?"

"Jah, but not today. I'll go by and tell her tomorrow."

"Do you want me to go with you?"

Hannah shook her head. "*Nee,* this is something I have to do by myself. You can't hold my hand for the rest of my life."

"I will if you need me to," Laney offered. "If you change your mind, swing by, and pick me up. I'm not doing anything special tomorrow except weeding the garden, and you know I'll do anything to get out of that chore!"

The mention of the garden made Hannah's thoughts turn to Eli's visit yesterday, and it made her start to cry all over again.

CHAPTER TWELVE

Eli unloaded the last of the hay bales into the Bishop's barn; he'd taken his time hoping he could avoid taking the meal with him and his family, but Cassie had come out to tell him they were holding the meal for him. Now, he rushed to get everything put away, so he didn't make them wait any longer. The Bishop had practically begged him to give Cassie a chance, and he'd tried to tell him he wasn't interested in her that way, but he'd almost insisted he give it some thought and take her for a buggy ride this evening. He wasn't interested in taking the girl for a buggy ride; he was in love with Hannah. At least he thought he was; her behavior today made him second-guess himself where she was concerned. She'd acted harsh and had even gloated over her win, and it hurt him significantly.

No matter how things ended up with Hannah, he was still not interested in Cassie and did not want to jump from one woman to the next. He needed a break to sort out his feelings and being pushed into taking a buggy ride with the Bishop's daughter was not a wise move for him at this stage in his life. When he'd been given the choice between Hannah and the ponies, he'd chosen her, and it would seem it had been the wrong decision. His mind was not in the right place to be making those types of decisions, but still, he had to abide by the Bishop's wishes even if he didn't agree with them.

He closed the barn door and went to the outside hose to clean his boots. He could leave them in the mudroom, but they would track mud all over, and he didn't want to make a mess for *Frau* Troyer to have to clean up. After his boots were hosed off, he splashed some of the cool water on his face and wet down his hair. It had been a long day in the hot sun, and he needed to cool off before he attempted to be sociable. He hadn't had the courage to tell the Bishop that he was falling for Hannah, but at the time he'd approached him about Cassie, his feelings were still too new for Hannah. He wished now that he would have said something because now that Hannah had broken his heart, he was in no condition emotionally to be put on the spot about courting Cassie. He didn't understand her obsession with him, especially since they'd never had any more conversation than greeting each other at Sunday services. He let out a heavy sigh and turned off the water; there was no sense in his trying to figure out women's ways. He'd certainly gotten it completely wrong where Hannah was concerned.

He pasted on a smile before entering the Bishop's home through the mudroom and pulled off his boots. Cassie turned around from the sink when he came into the kitchen.

"You can wash up in the bathroom; you know where it is."

He knew, but as far as he was concerned, he'd already washed up in the hose outside. He guessed that wasn't good enough in a woman's eyes, so he went to the washroom around the corner and used the soap. When he finished, he dragged himself back to the kitchen and sat across from the Bishop, who was reading this week's edition of *The Budget.*

The Bishop handed him a section, and he opened it, grateful for something to occupy his hands while Cassie and her mother bustled about the kitchen bringing food and dishes to the table. Though he held the newspaper in front of his face, his eyes trolled over the same sentence repeatedly; he was unable to think about anything except the look on Hannah's face when the Bishop had declared her the winner of the ponies. She was happy and glowing for the first few minutes until they made eye-contact. It was then that he'd seen her competitive side—a side of her he didn't care for.

When everything was ready, the Bishop put down his paper, and Eli folded his section and put it on the chair next to him, but Cassie removed it and sat down, moving the chair too close to him for his comfort. She was not going to make this easy for him; he was going to have to let her down easy because he could tell she was not going to take no for an answer too readily.

The Bishop bowed his head, and he could feel Cassie slipping her hand in his; it made him feel uncomfortable, but he didn't pull his hand away for fear it would cause problems he wasn't prepared to address. When the prayer was over, he yanked his hand back from hers and put them in his lap until the food dishes were passed to him. His stomach was in knots, and he didn't feel up to eating, but he didn't want to insult the Bishop's wife, so when the ham and potato salad were passed to him, he put small portions on his plate.

"You can have more than that," Cassie said to him. "Surely you worked up an appetite with all that hard work you did today."

He forced a smile. "I think I got a little overheated out there in the sun, so I don't have much of an appetite, but it smells so *gut* I wish

I was hungrier. Perhaps once I cool off, I can have a second helping, *danki,* though."

"I get that way myself sometimes," the Bishop said, letting him off the hook. "You'll be starving by the time bedtime hits."

He nodded. "Probably."

"Well, I'm starving!" Cassie said.

"You've had quite the appetite lately," her mother whispered. "Best to mind your figure if you want to get a husband."

She put back two of the four slices of ham she'd piled on her plate. Eli had noticed she'd put on a little weight, but she had always been too thin in his opinion. Not that her weight or eating habits were any of his business, and he suddenly found himself wishing he hadn't heard her mother's comment. Eli didn't find it very kind, but he kept it to himself. The Bishop and his wife were known to be very strict, but he supposed they felt they needed to set the example for the community.

Eli took his time eating, trying to keep food in his mouth at all times so he wouldn't have to join in the conversation too much. After the morning he'd had, he wasn't feeling very sociable. Not only that, but his stomach was so twisted with worry about the Bishop's request that he take Cassie for a buggy ride after the meal. Truth be told, all he wanted was a hot shower and his pillow for the next eight or so hours, but he'd agreed reluctantly to the man's request. It had felt more like an order than a request, but he prayed it would have a good outcome. It was in God's hands now; all he felt was helpless.

Before too long, Cassie was bounding from her chair and began to clear the table. "Would you like dessert now or would you like to wait until after our buggy ride?" she asked him.

"I'm too full for dessert," he said, sliding his plate to her outstretched hand. "Maybe another time."

He didn't intend to come back into the house after the buggy ride. He didn't even intend to take her far. Eli didn't believe she would want to be out with him long after he let her down and rejected her, but he had no other choice but to let her down as easy as he possibly could. He couldn't let her or the Bishop believe there was any hope for a future between them; he wasn't sure if he'd ever feel the same after the way Hannah broke his heart today.

"I'm ready to go, then," she announced with a bright smile.

Eli looked to the Bishop to bail him out, but he'd already put his nose back in his newspaper and didn't look up from it. He was on his own, and that worried him.

He followed the eager girl out to his buggy, suddenly regretting bringing his open buggy this morning. What had he been thinking? If anyone saw them together, they'd get the wrong idea. Perhaps he could stay on the back roads and avoid the busier ones. The only problem was, he had to go dangerously close to Hannah's road to go any further than the one they were on currently. He let out a sigh hoping he could explain if necessary, but what did it matter when it all came down to it? She didn't want him anymore; she'd proved that by her actions today.

When they exited her driveway, Cassie scooted closer to him, and it made him uncomfortable. "Someone might get the wrong idea about us if you don't move back over to your side of the seat," he said firmly.

She looped her arm in his and leaned her head on his shoulder. "I want them to get that idea; we're out on a buggy ride, after all. What's to confuse them?"

"I need to be honest with you, Cassie," Eli said with a shaky voice. "I'm only taking you for an evening drive to show my appreciation for feeding me after a hard day of work in your *vadder's* field. I am not taking you for a buggy ride; I don't want you to misunderstand."

"But *mei dat* said you were happy to take me for a buggy ride, so I thought…"

"I mean no disrespect to your *vadder,*" Eli interrupted her. "But he's the Bishop, and people have a tough time saying no when he makes a request. I agreed to be polite; I'm not interested in you. I'm in love with someone else."

Cassie began to cry, and he didn't know what to do.

"I'm sorry," he said. "I didn't mean to hurt your feelings."

"Nee, it's not you; I *have* to get married."

"You *have* to?" No sooner than he asked the question than it dawned on him why. *"Ach,* I'm so sorry about your trouble, Cassie, and normally, I'd do the honorable thing and offer to marry you, but I can't when I feel so strongly about Hannah."

"Hannah?" she asked. "You're in love with Hannah? I didn't think she even liked you at all—I mean after what happened today. I thought you two were merely competing."

"Nee, I love her, but you're right about how things turned out today; I'm not so sure she feels the same about me."

"If she doesn't, will you at least consider me?" she was practically begging, and it broke Eli's heart for her.

He smiled sadly after turning his buggy around. "*Jah,* I'll consider it, but if I don't, I'll help you in any way I can."

She placed a short kiss on his cheek and smiled through her tears. "*Danki,* that means a lot to me."

Eli drove Cassie back to her house, thanking God his troubles weren't as bad as hers were.

CHAPTER THIRTEEN

Hannah waited for her parents to leave to go over to see her uncle before she hitched up her horse and left the house to go see the matchmaker. She'd made excuses to her parents about supper last night and again at breakfast this morning. Though her stomach growled, she'd not wanted to sit with them and have to explain things repeatedly. She'd grabbed a muffin off the counter and stuffed it in her mouth now as she took her time driving to Miss Sadie's house. She was in no hurry to tell her she couldn't get the matched ponies after all. If there was a way for her to take them back to Ohio with her she would, but they would have to pack only what they could carry with them on the Greyhound bus. Everything else would have to stay behind.

After two bites of the muffin, she was feeling more like she'd swallowed a couple of rocks and they weighed down her stomach. She tossed it over into the grass on the side of the road, thinking a raccoon would probably find it and have himself a delightful breakfast. All Hannah knew was that she couldn't take another bite for fear that it would come back up.

She rode along thinking of what she was going to say to the matchmaker; it was a pleasant morning, one that she would typically enjoy. Not today; no amount of chirping birds was going to put her in a good mood. Not even the butterflies that floated atop the fields amused her this morning. They simply reminded her of the butterflies she missed that Eli had put in her stomach. How could she have been such a fool to think he loved her? It made her angry that she'd kissed him so passionately, but she'd fallen in love with him; what were his reasons for kissing her with such passion? Surely, if he'd meant it when he kissed her, he couldn't have fallen out of love for her that quickly. Had she done something wrong? Was it the competition over the ponies that had ended things between them?

She blew out a breath; she was not going to take responsibility for this—at least not all of it. She could admit she'd become too competitive over them, and for some men that could probably be a big turnoff. Perhaps she should have simply let it go from the very beginning; maybe then she'd at least have Eli. Now, she was left with nothing; it had all been for nothing.

When she pulled into the matchmaker's driveway, she found her weeding her garden— something Hannah herself would have been doing today if she wasn't leaving the community. She hopped down and strolled toward the woman, her heart beating so hard it felt as if it was trying to free itself from the confinement of her ribcage. She knew how it felt; she was screaming to get out of the community and couldn't get out fast enough.

Miss Sadie looked up at her and smiled. "The ponies are in the corral if you want to go see them; while you're down there, I can go in and wash up and get us something cool to drink so we can talk for a little bit."

She nodded and forced a smile. "*Danki,* I would like to see them for a few minutes."

Hannah walked toward the corral and a lump formed in her throat when she spotted them. They came toward the fence to greet her the way they always did, and it almost broke her heart to think she wasn't going to see them again. They'd gotten so used to her; they were almost like her pets, and she would miss them so much. She was looking forward to watching them grow and saddle breaking them when they were old enough. She was looking forward to riding them, and now she wouldn't be a part of their lives. Now, she feared the new owner, if it wasn't going to be Eli, would harness train them too soon. Not many farmers could afford to keep a couple of hay burners in their corral until they were old enough to pull a buggy. She felt sorry for them; could she stay here just to protect them?

She patted them on the neck and smoothed out their manes. "I'm going to miss you both," she said with a shaky voice. "After today, you probably won't see me again; I'm really sorry I can't get you and raise you, but I pray that your new owners will be *gut* to you."

Tears welled up from her throat and dripped down her cheeks. She stood there for a few minutes watching them canter around the pen; they were fine-looking ponies, and she would miss seeing them grow into even more beautiful horses once they were full grown.

Unable to bear looking at them any longer, she walked back toward the yard where Miss Sadie was waiting for her with a pitcher of lemonade and a plate full of cookies. That was something you could always count on from the woman; she loved to entertain and always had plenty of refreshments on hand for drop-in guests. Her stomach growled, reminding her she hadn't had more than the two bites of the muffin on the way here, but she feared eating anything on her nervous stomach. She would gladly accept a glass of the lemonade though since she hadn't thought to get anything to drink. Though she would prefer coffee, it was too hot in the morning sun already to drink anything hot out here.

She sat across from the matchmaker, her jittery insides knotting up in a hard rock in her gut. "I have something I need to tell you before I chicken out," Hannah blurted out.

"What is wrong?" the matchmaker asked. "You look upset; you should be happy you won the ponies."

"About that," she began. "I can't take them."

"Why not? You won the competition."

"I know, but I'm leaving the community."

"What about Eli? Does he know?" the matchmaker asked.

"*Nee,* why would I tell him?"

"I thought the two of you were in love."

"You thought wrong!" Hannah barked. "I thought he loved me too, but it turns out he was only trying to—I don't know what he was trying to do, but it wasn't the truth whatever it was."

She knew she sounded angry and wasn't making any sense—not even to herself, but she was suddenly more confused than ever.

"Eli came here to talk to me the night before last," Miss Sadie said.

"With Cassie," Hannah interrupted.

The matchmaker shook her head, confusion in her expression. "*Nee,* he didn't come here with Cassie, but I did ask him to give her a ride home because it was getting dark and she'd walked over. He was kind enough to take her, so I didn't have to hitch up my buggy and take her myself."

Hannah was confused; if he didn't come here with her to make a match, then why was he here? Did she dare ask?

"I can see in your face you want to know what he was doing here," Miss Sadie said. "He was very upset about the competition. He let you win the cake competition, you know."

"I thought that too!" Hannah said. "Why did he do that when my cake was too salty?"

The matchmaker smiled kindly. "He didn't want to break your confidence as a woman; he said your cooking skills were more important to you as a woman than they are to him as a *mann;* he is a very wise young *mann,* that Eli is."

"I guess he figured he wouldn't embarrass me so I could get a husband since he's marrying Cassie!"

Miss Sadie let a chuckle escape her lips. "What makes you think he's marrying Cassie?"

"Because she told me he almost kissed her after he took her home and that they were going to be married."

Sadie sighed and shook her head. "You young people make so many more problems for yourselves than you need to. Cassie came over here begging me to match her with Eli, but I told her no because I already had someone else in mind for him—you, Hannah."

"Well, that didn't work out; even if he's not marrying Cassie, I messed everything up by competing with him for the ponies."

"Which brings me to Eli's visit; he spoke to me privately while Cassie stayed on the porch and he asked me to give you the ponies because he didn't want to humiliate you by competing with you in the hay baling."

"Because he loves Cassie?"

The matchmaker scoffed. *"Nee,* because he loves *you!"*

Hannah's breath hitched. She felt as if her heart had stopped; she was numb, and the lump in her throat wouldn't go down. How could she have been such a fool to think he would take up with the likes of Cassie Troyer? She hadn't trusted him even for a minute; her mother had warned her to trust him, and she hadn't.

"He can have the ponies," Hannah sobbed. "I'm sure he doesn't love me now that I rubbed it in his face that I won. I acted like a spoiled child having Cassie help me so I could beat him at the hay baling. I could see how tired he was, but I didn't care; I was so mad at him for something that I *thought* he did that I didn't see he needed me to give up the fight. Why didn't you say something to me before the competition?"

"It wasn't my place," she said gently. "I thought he was going to tell you, but I guess he didn't get the chance."

"I didn't give him a chance!" Hannah cried. "I marched up to the flatbed and announced Cassie was going to help me win, never stopping to even say hello to him. He must think I hate him. What am I going to do?"

"I guess you'll have to tell him how you feel and that you made a mistake," the matchmaker said.

"I can't; I'm too much of a coward!" Hannah cried. "If he turned me away, I'd probably die of embarrassment."

"You're being a little bit dramatic; don't you think?" Miss Sadie asked.

"Just promise me that you'll let him have the ponies," Hannah begged her. "He earned them rightfully. Not only was his cake better than mine, but I took advantage of him when he was tired and had Cassie help me with the hay baling, which wasn't fair to him. I haven't been fair to him this whole time, and he's been more than fair to me. Any *mann* who would take a loss just to spare my feelings and then come to you and tell you to give me the ponies deserves a woman who will treat him better than I did. I love him but obviously not enough. So please; give him the ponies. I don't want them anymore because they would only remind me of how selfish I am."

Sadie smiled. "I would have to say that giving up your rights to the ponies and wanting Eli to have them is a very unselfish thing; I commend you for that. It shows maturity."

"It's a little too late, don't you think?"

"*Nee,* it's never too late to do the right thing," the matchmaker said.

"I would much rather have Eli's love than those ponies, but my selfishness cost me both of them."

"Why don't you talk to him; tell him how you feel."

"Nee, if I was him, I wouldn't want to hear anything I had to say," Hannah said.

"Eli is a *gut* young *mann,"* Sadie said. "I'm sure he would listen."

"You don't have to tell me what a *gut mann* he is," Hannah said. "I just wish I would have realized that before it was too late. It's too late to fix things with him. Let him have the ponies; I'll be leaving in a few days—with or without my parents. If they want to stay, I have a friend I can go stay with, but I think it's better if I leave the community."

"You will be missed," Sadie said.

Though Hannah appreciated the matchmaker saying that, somehow, she doubted anyone would miss her after the fool she'd made of herself. She was certain everyone knew about it already, and she'd be laughed at for years to come. No, she wasn't up for that; it was best if she went away with what little dignity she had left.

CHAPTER FOURTEEN

Hannah silently packed her things as she sniffled back the tears that threatened to reopen her floodgates. Her parents had decided they did not want to leave the community but had agreed that as a grown woman, she could be out on her own. Her friend, Katie Lantz, back in Ohio would take her in. Her family owned a bakery where she could work; Katie lived in the loft apartment above the bakery, and she would room with her there. It was what was best. After the spectacle she'd made of herself and her competing over the ponies, no man would want to marry her here. The best she could hope for would be that the rumors of her behavior would take a while to catch up to her in her old community and she would be able to find someone eventually—once her broken heart mended. If it ever did. She loved Eli even more if that was possible, and it hurt to even think about him. After the matchmaker told her of his unselfishness with her about the ponies, she learned too late that she should have trusted him.

"No sense crying over spilled milk, *Mamm* always says," she said, sniffling.

A knock on her door startled her, and she hollered, *"Come in!"* thinking it was only Laney.

Hannah wiped her cheeks hastily when Cassie walked into her room.

"I know you're surprised to see me, but I could really use a friend," Cassie said, quietly.

"As you can see, I'm packing to leave," Hannah said. "I'm going back to Ohio."

"I'm going to be honest with you about something, Hannah; I asked Eli to marry me. He agreed to think about it."

Hannah sank to the edge of her bed; she couldn't breathe, and her heart raced. Sweat formed on her brow, and her hands shook.

"You look like you're going to be sick," Cassie said.

"He'll make you a fine husband and a *gut* provider," Hannah said with a shaky voice.

"I think you love him!" Cassie said. "I don't blame you; he's everything you said and more. He has a kind heart."

She looked up at Cassie, her eyes filled with tears. "I wish you the best in your new life with Eli."

"Nee, I can't marry him when his heart belongs to you; he would never love me as much as he loves you."

Hannah blinked away tears. "What are you talking about?"

"When I asked him if he'd marry me," Cassie began. "He told me that normally he'd help me out, but he was in love with someone else and didn't know how she felt about him. Then he admitted that *someone* was *you*; if you

166

love him the way I think you do; you should tell him."

"I can't; it's too late for all that," Hannah said. "I made a fool of myself."

Cassie smirked. "You didn't make as big a fool of yourself as I did; I practically threw myself at him out of desperation. I'm so sorry."

"Don't be sorry," Hannah said. "Why did you do it?"

Cassie barely looked up at her. "Why does any woman throw herself at a *mann* and beg him to marry her?"

Hannah shrugged.

"I'm in the *familye* way."

"*Ach,* I'm so sorry; I mean congratulations. What does your *familye* think about that?"

"I know you don't know how to react; I'm so scared. *Mei familye* doesn't know about it, and I'm sure as soon as *mei vadder* finds out, he'll send me away."

"I'd be scared too! What are you going to do about the *boppli?*" Hannah asked. "Will you keep it or give it up for adoption?"

Cassie shrugged. "I'd like to keep it, but I don't have any way of supporting it. *Mei vadder* will surely shun me when he finds out. Or he'll send me away until I give birth and then make me come back to the community without *mei boppli* just to keep himself from embarrassment. He's a very strict *mann.*"

"If I had a way for you to keep your *boppli* and keep from being shunned by your *familye,* would you do it?"

Her face brightened. "*Jah,* but how will I hide a *boppli* from *mei familye*? I'm already starting to put on weight and *mei mudder* has been lecturing me about keeping my figure to land a husband. She said something about it in front of Eli, and I was so embarrassed."

"You won't have to hide it. I was going to stay with my friend, Katie," Hannah said. "Her *familye* owns a bakery, and she lives above it in the loft apartment. It has two bedrooms; I was going to live there with her and work at the bakery, but if I'm going to stay here and try to work things out with Eli, you could take my place. It seems like you need to get away more than I do, and Katie would love the company. She would dote on you and the *boppli* and help with it in any way she could. They have a much less strict *Ordnung* than this community so you'll fit right in."

Cassie teared up. "You would do that for me?"

Hannah pulled her into a hug. "You came here looking for a friend, and you got one; you'll have two when you meet Katie. The two of you will get along like peanut butter and strawberry jam!"

"I don't deserve a friend like you," Cassie said, her gaze downcast. "I have to admit I came here to lie to you. I was going to tell you that Eli was the *vadder* of *mei boppli* so you would not pursue him and I could marry him. He said he would think about it if things didn't work out with the two of you, but I didn't have the heart to tell you such a lie after seeing how much the two of you love each other. "I'm so sorry I was going to lie to you out of desperation; I'm scared though and having a *mann* like Eli rescue me from shaming *mei vadder* was all I could think about."

"I understand, and I'm not upset with you; I'd be terrified if I was in your place. I'm grateful to you because honestly, not many women would give up what they want for the sake of someone else. You've done me a favor as a friend, and now I'm going to do a favor for you because I think we could both use a friend right now. Let me call Katie at the bakery and tell her I changed my mind and that you'll be taking my place; is it alright if I do that?"

Cassie shook her head and smiled sadly. "*Jah,* I really need a friend right now, and I'm grateful for any help you can give me."

Hannah looked at the stuff she had begun to pack. "I guess I can unpack now and tell *mei mudder* I'm staying; she's going to be so happy."

"I'm so happy for you; you're a lucky woman to have a *mann* like Eli."

"I don't have him yet!" Hannah said. "I'm going to have to eat a whole humble pie before I can convince him I'm the right woman for him. But thanks to you opening my eyes, I think I can try. If it doesn't work out, then at least I can't say I didn't give it everything I have."

"Just be honest with him and tell him you lost your focus," Cassie said. "He's a *gut mann,* and I'm sure he'll give you another chance."

"I don't know," she said. "I messed up pretty badly. I let him take a loss for the cake baking when his cake was better than mine, and then I practically rubbed his nose in the loss over the hay baling. I acted like a horrible person."

"Everyone deserves a second chance," Cassie said. "I hope someday I'll get a second chance with someone as wonderful as your Eli is. You're a lucky woman."

Hannah had to admit she felt luckier than Cassie probably did at this time in her life. She suddenly realized she had a lot to be grateful for; at least she wasn't faced with the same troubles as Cassie was right now. The poor woman had a long and troubled road ahead of her, but if anyone could help her to make things right, it was her friend Katie in Ohio.

"If you want me to, I can take you to the bus station tomorrow," Hannah said. "You can use my ticket since I'm not going to use it."

"*Danki,* I appreciate it," Cassie said. "I don't have any money to get there. I hate to sneak away, but perhaps in time, my parents will understand. I guess I'll have to leave them a note; I'm too big of a coward to tell them the truth about what I'm going through right now. I don't exactly understand it myself so there's no way I could try to explain to them."

"You didn't do too badly explaining it to me," Hannah said. "If you want me to, I'd be happy to sit with you when you tell them. That is if you want to talk to them before you leave."

"I think it's best if they think I'm going away on *rumspringa,*" Cassie said. "They would probably accept that easier, and I'll have the excuse I need to get away after Eli rejected me."

Hannah nodded. "I was using the same excuse, and my parents bought it, so I'm sure yours will, but I wish you'd consider telling them the truth. They might surprise you by supporting you."

She shook her head. "*Nee,* when my *schweschder,* Abby found herself in the same situation, *mei vadder* forced her into a marriage with a *mann* she didn't love just so she could cover up the pregnancy. He wasn't even the *vadder,* but he was willing to marry her. I know the *mann* he would force me to marry, and I'm not going to stick around to let him do that to me. Not when I can see how miserable Abby is."

"Who would he make you marry?" Hannah was truly curious.

"The widower, Abraham Glick!" Cassie said with a shudder.

"That *mann* is twice your age!" Hannah said. "He has a *dochder* your age—Ellen."

"*Jah,* I know, but that would be his choice for me; I can't stay here and marry a *mann* that old. I'd be miserable. He's not a kind *mann.* I don't believe he's a widower; I think his *fraa* ran away!"

Hannah let a giggle escape her lips and quickly covered her mouth to contain it. "I think I agree with you."

Cassie laughed. "I don't remember going to the funeral, do you? I think she just sort of disappeared one day."

Hannah shook her head. "I don't remember it either," she said. "I'm curious about something—if I'm not prying by asking, but does the *vadder* of your *boppli* know he's going to be a *vadder?* Can you get him to help you at all?"

Cassie shook her head with downcast eyes. "He's an *Englisher* I met a couple of months ago; I tried the phone number he gave me, and they said I had the wrong number. I went to the apartment where he lived, and they said he doesn't live there anymore and don't know where he is. He dumped me a couple of days *after* and I haven't seen him since. He

174

said he just wondered what it would be like to *be with* an Amish girl and he doesn't love me and didn't want to date me anymore. He said I satisfied his curiosity, and that's all; it really hurt me, but I've forgiven him."

"*Ach,* I'm so sorry he treated you that way; I don't know if I would be able to forgive him that easily."

"It wasn't easy, but I think it's best that way because I don't want to be bitter about the *boppli,*" she said. "They are a blessing and a gift from *Gott,* and I know he has a reason for blessing me with this *boppli* even though it wasn't conceived in his will."

"*Gott* still loves you; his love for us is unconditional, so enjoy your blessing and raise it in his will. *Gott* will continue to bless you."

Cassie smiled. "He already has by blessing me with your friendship and giving me the chance to go away and keep this *boppli.*"

Hannah hugged Cassie feeling very blessed herself at the moment.

CHAPTER FIFTEEN

Hannah walked in through the kitchen door and hugged her mother.

"What's this all about?" she asked. "I haven't offered you any of these warm cookies yet!"

"I just wanted to thank you for being such an understanding *mudder,* and to tell you that I love you," Hannah gushed.

"I love you too, Hannah, you know that."

She nodded. "I do, and I'm lucky to have you."

"Does this have anything to do with you giving Cassie your bus ticket to Ohio?" her mother asked, dishing up a plate of cookies from the cooling rack.

"*Jah,*" Hannah said, taking the plate from her and taking it to the table.

Her mother grabbed the milk from the refrigerator and two cups and sat across from her after pouring them each a glass.

"Her parents agreed to let her go to Ohio, but not without a fight; the Bishop was trying to make her marry that old *mann* widower, Abe Glick! She had to threaten she'd run away and never come back before he agreed to give her a chance to go out on her own, but he agreed she needed to leave if she refused to marry that old *mann.*"

"*Ach,* I feel sorry for her, but Katie's *familye* will be *gut* to her and the *boppli;* I appreciate you talking to me about all of this last night when you told me you were staying home. I'm so happy you're staying, but now what are you going to do about Eli? I think Cassie's advice to you was sound advice, don't you?"

She nodded, stuffing a cookie in her mouth and chewing it before answering.

"I agree, but I think I want to give things a few days to quiet down," she said. "It would probably be a *gut* idea if I spent some time in prayer, so I don't mess things up more with him. I want to be sure I say the right thing to him this time. I know I hurt him and if I give him some time to heal from that it might be easier on both of us if I don't push him."

"You're growing up to be a wise young woman," her mother said.

Buggy wheels, followed by multiple whinnying from horses brought them from the table to the kitchen window.

"What's he doing here?" Hannah asked. "And why does he have the ponies with him? You don't suppose he's here to rub it in my face, do you?"

Her mother shook her head. "You know better than that, but if he is, you need to go take your medicine."

Hannah sighed. "I guess you're right; whatever he says to me, I completely deserve every bit of it after the way I treated him. I guess I'll have to give him my apology now even though I wasn't ready yet."

"I can talk to him if you want me to— until you're ready," her mother offered.

"Nee, I better get this over with—part of me being that grownup woman you were just talking about."

Her mother pulled her into a hug. "Whatever happens, you know that it's *Gott's* will."

She nodded. "I know."

Hannah went outside to greet Eli; she pasted on a smile and approached him. He'd unhitched the ponies from the back of his buggy and faced her.

Without warning, he handed her the leather straps connected to their bits and bent down on one knee before her.

Hannah's breath hitched.

"I want you to share these ponies with me—as *mei fraa*—if you'll have me," he said, looking up at her with smiling blue eyes. "I love you, Hannah and I want you to marry me."

A half-giggle, half-cry escaped her lips. "*Jah,*" she gushed. "I'm so sorry for the way I acted; I love you, and I want to be your *fraa.*"

Eli rose from bended knee and pulled her into his arms. "Is it okay if I kiss you right out here in your driveway?"

She nodded, and he pressed his lips to hers in a simple and quick kiss. "None of that other stuff matters, Hannah. When the matchmaker brought the ponies over to *mei haus* this morning and told me you had said for her to give them to me and that you were leaving the community, I was so afraid I would lose you forever!"

"I didn't go; I'm not going," she said. "I sent Cassie in my place."

"Cassie?"

"Jah," Hannah said. "She came over here yesterday and told me what you said to her; I think it was an honorable thing you did, offering to help her even though it wasn't your responsibility. She told me that you loved me and she couldn't marry you and stand between us—not after I told her how much I love you too. So I gave her my bus ticket and took her to the bus station after helping her tell her parents about her troubles. They weren't very understanding of her situation, but they agreed to let her go to Ohio for a fresh new start. She was right when she told me what a *gut mann* you are and how worthy you were to pursue. I'm lucky to have you."

"I'm the lucky one," he said. "I should have never agreed to compete with you; it wasn't fair to you when the matchmaker had promised these ponies to you a couple of years ago. I should have let it go then instead of insisting she give me a chance to buy them."

"You did anyway," Hannah said with a giggle.

"Actually, I didn't buy them."

"Did *mei vadder* get them instead?"

"Nee, the matchmaker gave them to us as a wedding present—well, she said as long as you said yes to my proposal, but I told her I'd do my best to convince you."

Hannah giggled. "She gave them to us? Gosh, I feel so blessed. Not just for the ponies, but for you, too!"

"I feel blessed too, but I'm not looking forward to going over to the Bishop's *haus* and having to reload all of that hay I just stacked in his barn for him to sell," Eli said. "I'm going to have to purchase the entire barn full to feed these two hay burners."

Hannah laughed. "Don't worry, I'll help you; I'm a champion at hay baling!"

He chuckled. "You know, I think I heard that from someone!"

She nudged him playfully. "Don't remind me!"

182

"Hey, you're the one who brought it up; I'm going to hold you to that promise because that's a lot of hay."

"I will help you with the hay bales, I promise," she said, petting the ponies' necks. "I'll do anything for these two beauties—and for you, of course."

"I love how you put that into perspective!" he said with a chuckle.

She kissed him on the cheek. "Don't worry; you'll always come first in my life. I'd rather have you over these ponies—but I'm sure glad I can have both!"

"Me too!" he said with a bright smile.

"I do have one question for you," she said.

"What's that?"

"Why did you let the cake baking be a tie instead of taking the win and letting it all be over with?"

"Because I didn't want to starve my entire married life with you by insulting your cake," he said with a smirk.

She threw her head back and laughed, and he joined her.

"Just promise me something," he said. "Next time you make *mei mudder's* cake, you'll go easy on the salt."

"I'm vowing right now never to make your *mudder's* cake again; if you want one, you'll have to bake it, or we'll get her to do the baking for us!"

Eli nodded. "Fair enough!"

Hannah helped Eli hitch the ponies up to the back of his buggy, and they took them to his corral where they would live out the rest of their days being pampered. As for Hannah, she couldn't wait to marry Eli so he could pamper her too.

THE END

Other Book series by Samantha Bayarr

Amish Ever After series:

Amish Sweethearts: The Amish Portrait

Amish Sweethearts: The English Cousin

Amish Sweethearts: Amish Wedding Season

Amish Acres series:

The Celery Patch

Tobacco Rows

The Pumpkin Patch

Sunflower Meadow

Wild Honeysuckle

Amish Homecoming series:

Amish Proposal

Amish Auction

Amish Promise

Amish Outcast

Amish Hearts series:

Her Amish Heart

Her Amish Love (coming soon)

You might also like:

Please enjoy the sample chapters of

HER AMISH HEART

Her Amish Heart

Copyright © Samantha Bayarr 2019

Scripture quotations are from New King James Version of the Bible.

CHAPTER ONE

SOPHIE Webber planted her hands on her hips defiantly and looked her father straight in the eye as if to stand her ground. "I can't go an entire summer without my cellphone or my computer," she argued. "How will I talk to my friends?"

"You can send them a letter!" her father said.

"You mean like—in the mail?" she squealed. "I only have their phone numbers and email addresses. They'd laugh at me if I sent them a letter in the mail."

Her father scowled at her from around his newspaper. "If they'd laugh at you over something that simple, then you can't really count them as very good friends, can you?"

Tears welled up in Sophie's eyes as she sat in the chair across from him at the breakfast table. "But Dad! You said all I had to do was finish college to get my trust fund; why are you putting another condition on it when I already did as you asked me to do?"

"You're twenty-five years old, and that's too old to argue with me like a child," he reprimanded her. "You might have finished college, but there isn't much you can do with a Liberal Arts Degree, and I'm not convinced you've grown up. Spending the summer helping someone other than yourself will help you grow up, and this is the best way; to go away and learn about a slower way of life."

"More like the nineteenth century!" Sophie complained. "The Amish are so slow; they're a backward society. If you want me to experience other cultures, why do I have to do that in an Amish community? You could send me to Hawaii instead; I could learn a lot from the natives there!"

Hugh Webber folded his newspaper with a snap and glared at his daughter. Mrs. Hildebrand, their cook, placed a plate of poached eggs and toast in front of him and he set the newspaper on the table. He took a sip from the coffee the woman refilled for him before he resumed their conversation.

"I've made up my mind," Hugh said with a firmness his daughter didn't care for. "I should have done this years ago—long before you became so spoiled. You need to learn a few life-lessons. Things I can't teach you. I've spoiled you with a cook and a housekeeper, and you don't even know how to boil water or sew on a button. The Amish can teach you those things better than anyone, and it won't cost me like your expensive, private school, and the countless musical lessons, riding lessons, and dance lessons you gave up on too easily."

Sophie pushed back the bowl of fresh fruit in front of her and folded her arms over her middle. "I don't need to know how to sew a button," she said. "I can just buy a new blouse!"

Hugh put down his forkful of eggs and wagged his finger at his daughter. "That's exactly the mentality that caused me to finally make this decision; you don't know the value of hard work. You don't even understand the concept of how to survive without servants and cooks."

"I just finished college: that's hard work!" she protested. "And I had to go without a cook and a housekeeper the whole time I was there."

He pursed his lips and scowled. "That doesn't count; you ate takeout the entire time, and if I remember, your roommate had her housekeeper come in and clean your dorm once a week! There's a whole world out there you know nothing about, Sophie. You need to mature so you don't end up spending your trust fund on frivolous things that will leave you bankrupt in less than a year. Taking this job is the *only* way you're getting access to your trust fund—and only *after* the summer is over. If your mother was alive, she'd..." his voice trailed off.

Sophie leaned forward, eager for him to finish his sentence. "She'd what, Dad?"

He looked away without answering her.

Silence fell between them, and her father picked up his newspaper and held it in front of his face. It was what he did every time he *almost* spoke of her mother. It had been that way all her life, and Sophie couldn't understand why he wouldn't talk about her. She knew the pain in his eyes and his voice when he tried to talk about her. Sophie wished she could remember more about her mother than the few foggy memories that didn't amount to much, and she couldn't understand her father's reluctance to share things about her. She knew her father still missed her mother, but it was tough for Sophie to miss a mother she didn't remember having.

She reached over and touched her father's arm lightly; she hated the silence between them. "Tell me how you found the job for me," she almost begged. It wasn't what she wanted to talk about, but she couldn't stand it when he shut her out.

He lowered his newspaper, letting it rest across his plate. "I was taking a drive out in the country—we used to live on a farm when you were little; do you remember that?"

Sophie picked at the blueberry muffin in front of her and shrugged her shoulders. "Not really; didn't we move here when I was five?"

Hugh gave a curt nod, letting her know not to take the conversation any further toward talk of her mother. Through bits and pieces of conversations over the years, she'd learned they'd lived on a farm, but they'd moved to the city after her mother's funeral. She was only five years old at the time, and she had only a vague hint of a memory of the funeral.

"I met an Amish man while I was out there looking around; his name is Simon Yoder," her father said.

Sophie resisted the urge to roll her eyes; weren't all Amish people named *Yoder?*

"He's a nice fellow—a widower, and his mother recently suffered a mild stroke, and he needs help while she recovers because she can't take care of his two young daughters until she gets some physical therapy."

"Why would he want *me* to take care of his daughters?" Sophie asked. "I don't know anything about kids! And who does the cooking and cleaning?"

Hugh cleared his throat. "*You* will."

"Me?" she squealed. "I don't know how to cook anything!"

"You'll learn," he said with a calm reassurance she wasn't buying.

Sophie tossed her napkin on her plate. "It would take months of lessons from the finest chefs to teach me how to boil water!"

"Simon has assured me his mother can teach you."

"How is she supposed to teach me when she can't take care of the kids?"

Hugh gave his paper a snap to crease the middle and folded it once more, placing it next to his plate. Sophie gulped; experience warned her he was losing his patience with her and she'd be doing herself a favor if she closed her mouth and listened or this *punishment* was only going to get worse.

"The woman can still talk," her father said. "She has some paralysis on one side and can't walk very well, and she can't lift anything. But she still has all her faculties, and she will be there to instruct you on everything."

"I don't want her breathing down my neck all day watching everything I do!" Sophie said. "Oh, Dad, this is going to be the worst summer of my life—worse than the time you sent me to summer camp with all those dirty kids!"

"Those kids weren't dirty—they were *normal* kids who were underprivileged and didn't have designer clothes to wear the way you do," he said firmly.

"Like the Amish!" she said with an eye-roll. "Don't they sew their clothes out of flour sacks or something?"

Her father let out a low growling sigh. It was time for her to be quiet.

"If I recall, you had fun at that camp and didn't even want to come home at the end of the two weeks!" Hugh said. "Who knows, you might feel the same way about living among the Amish for a few months."

"Not likely!" she mumbled.

****

Sophie searched through her walk-in closet full of designer clothes, mourning the loss of them. She would miss them and her collection of designer shoes and purses her father ordered her to leave behind while she packed for her summer job.

This isn't going to be just a job; it's going to be a punishment, too!

His instructions had been simple enough; either she takes the job at the Amish farm, or she could kiss her trust fund goodbye. Why had he thought to choose the worst possible job for her? He'd given her a lecture about teaching her life lessons that she didn't learn while she was away at school, *blah-blah-blah.* She'd stopped listening to him after he informed her she had to leave her cell phone and laptop behind. The final blow had come when he'd presented her with the awful *uniform* she was to wear. It seemed that the Amish family *loaned* her a used dress and apron to wear, and a pair of black shoes she wouldn't be caught dead in. Even though the housekeeper had laundered the dress for her, the dress was still dingy and brown—like a potato sack—and it smelled like a barn!

Her father had seemed a little harsh when he'd explained that if she wanted more than one dress, she had to learn to sew it herself. She couldn't imagine trying to sew a dress; of course, the dress they'd given her was quite primitive. She supposed if she had to, she could trace around the material and cut out a pattern from that. She doubted they used patterns like the rest of the world.

Sophie let out a discouraging sigh; everything she was allowed to take with her didn't even fill a backpack.

She slumped down on the edge of her bed; she was grateful all her friends would be vacationing in nice places over the summer and wouldn't really have time for her anyway. She was certainly jealous of them, but at least she wouldn't be embarrassed by having to explain her plans to her friends.

Reclining onto her down feather comforter, she wished she could smuggle it into her backpack—that and her pillows.

They'll probably make me sleep in the barn, and I'll smell like cows and pigs all day!

Then a thought occurred to her; Kyle was the only person she knew who wasn't going away for the summer, and that was because he worked at his father's used-car lot. She hated to ask him for a favor because she was trying to cut ties with him, but she needed someone to bail her out in case things weren't going well. With no communication with the outside world, she needed an out—just in case.

She dialed Kyle's number, and he picked up on the first ring.

"Hey, I was just getting ready to call you to see if you wanted to go to the beach with me for the weekend," he said. "My buddies rented a condo, and they want me to go in with them, but you know I never have any money."

Sophie sighed; he was always asking her for money this way—without really asking her. It annoyed her that he thought she was an ATM or something.

"How much do you need?" she asked sarcastically.

"I don't want you to pay," he said, stumbling over his words. "I wanted you to go with me—you know—as my guest."

"You know I won't go anywhere with you unless I could have my own room," she said.

"When are you going to stop teasing me and stop saving yourself for marriage?"

Sophie bit her bottom lip to keep from calling him a jerk; she called him because she needed his help, and arguing with him and calling him names would not get her anywhere.

"I can't go; my dad is making me take a summer job!"

"Doing what?" he asked.

She blew out a breath before answering, bracing herself for him to tease her.

"A nanny to some Amish kids."

He chuckled. "Are you serious?"

She sighed again. "Yes!"

He let out another chuckle. "Oh wow; that's rough!"

"I need someone to help me out of it in case I have to bail," she explained. "Will you help me?"

He laughed some more until it dawned on him that she needed his help.

"Okay, but it's going to cost you!"

CHAPTER TWO

After the humiliation of handing over her cell phone and laptop to her father, Sophie let herself into the passenger side of her father's car. She'd said a sad goodbye to her car too; he had forbidden her to drive herself to her new *job*. She was completely cut off until she passed his little test. After that, she'd be a free woman and could use her trust fund any way she pleased. Until then, she was angry with him and wasn't even sure she wanted to talk to him.

She stared out the window while the radio played classical jazz; her father knew it calmed her, but now it served to fill the quiet void between them. She squirmed in her seat a little and adjusted her seatbelt; this was almost as bad as riding in an elevator full of strangers while everyone ignored each other except to make pointless small-talk. Only, she and her father weren't even making small-talk. They were simply ignoring each other—or maybe it was just her. She only knew it was irritating her.

An hour into the trip, they pulled off the highway onto a rural road; how far had he driven to find this Amish farm? Was there a specific destination he'd had in mind the day he'd come across the Yoder place? If so, did it have anything to do with where they had lived? She'd asked him a time or two over the years, but she'd given up when he refused to discuss anything to do with their farm. Now that she was being forced to take the job as nanny to the Yoder children, she was curious why he was suddenly willing to hint around about the subject. But as always, he clammed up as soon as her prying went too far.

Sophie watched the landscape whizzing by, boredom overtaking her to the point she wished she could get out and walk. Ignoring her mix of emotions, she mindlessly thought about the inhabitants of the occasional farmhouse they passed and wondered if she was happy as a child when they lived on a farm. Would she find anything about farm life familiar to her when she arrived on the Yoder farm, or would it be awkward and difficult?

Sophie hugged her sides and leaned against the window, ignoring the uneasiness in her gut. She shouldn't have eaten breakfast before they left; coffee would have been enough, and it wouldn't have given her heartburn. She reached for her bottle of water in the center console and took a large sip.

Gulping it down with a whip of her head toward the passing farm, she nearly dropped the water bottle in her lap.

"Stop the car!" she squealed, gripping her father's arm.

"What's wrong?"

She didn't answer; her neck was craned behind her as she watched out the back window.

Hugh slowed down and pulled over onto the grassy shoulder of the country road, and Sophie jumped out and ran back toward the farm they'd passed. She slowed her pace, walking slowly through the tall grass, ignoring her father's voice calling after her. Instead, she focused her gaze on the jerky movement of the windmill. It squeaked with every turn and shifted from side to side, the smallest breeze animating it. She stopped in her tracks, the high grass waving and tickling against her bare calves.

What was it about that windmill that had her so mesmerized?

"Mamma!" She whispered.

A glimpse of her mother rushed over her, a flutter of contentment rising from her heart. She tried to hold onto the memory, but it left her just as swiftly as it filled her. Her heart raced as if she was still running. That was the strongest memory she'd ever had of her mother. Why couldn't she ever hold onto the memories for more than a passing moment? Bliss turned to gloom within seconds.

Her throat constricted; for the first time in her life, she was feeling something other than indifference about her mother. By the time her father caught up with her, a single tear had rolled down her cheek. She quickly swiped at it before turning around; the memory was gone, and she couldn't get it back.

She walked past her father toward the car with him on her heels demanding an explanation from her. Even if she could give him one, she wouldn't. He would shut her down and refuse to answer the myriad of questions that had plagued her since she'd learned to talk. She stomped her feet and pursed her lips; it wasn't fair for him to keep her mother from her.

When she reached the car, she collapsed onto the passenger's seat and slammed her door. When her father got in, she turned her head away and bit her bottom lip to keep the tears stinging the backs of her eyes from giving away what she was feeling. If he knew, he'd ask her what was wrong and then she'd have to tell him and put up with him clamming up about the subject.

No thanks!

He sat next to her in silence, and she could feel his eyes on her; he wanted an explanation from her, but she would not give him one no matter what.

"I wish you'd tell me what that was all about," he said.

"You wouldn't understand," she mumbled.

After a few minutes, he started the car and pulled back onto the asphalt, ribbons of road still ahead of them.

"Will you forgive me?" he asked, breaking the silence.

Her jaw clenched, and she let her head drop against the window.

"For what?" she mumbled. "Exiling me to Amish country, or for cutting me off?"

"For spoiling you," he said gently. "I made a promise to your mother…"

His voice trailed off, but she hadn't missed the crack in his voice when he mentioned her mother. She knew how much pain he was still in even after twenty years had elapsed since her mother had passed away. She'd just experienced a hint of what that loss felt like and could no more process her feelings about that than she could relate to her father's pain. Though she couldn't remember enough to feel strongly about her mother, it broke her heart that she'd been without her for her whole life. If she'd remembered more than the scant recollection of the woman, she might have a better understanding of what she should be feeling, but it was hard to miss something she didn't remember having.

What could she say now? Was her heart so hardened that she had lost compassion for her father? No! She turned around in her seat and placed a hand on his and gave it a gentle squeeze.

"When you come home," he said. "We'll talk, and I'll answer all your questions; promise me you'll give this job your best and keep an open mind about this."

She nodded reluctantly. "I'll try."

He slowed down the car and turned into a long driveway that led to a white clapboard farmhouse with black shutters. Sophie felt a familiarity about the place, but she kept it to herself; most of the farms they'd passed on the way over had the same general look about them. She stared at the house, her heart taking a faster pace. Her mouth felt dry, and her legs felt wobbly as she tried to get out of the car. She coughed when she breathed in deeply; how did people live with the animal smell without losing their breakfast every day?

She clamped a hand over her nose and mouth and groaned. Her father breathed in deeply and smiled.

"That's fresh air you're smelling!" he said cheerfully.

She shook her head and frowned, her eyes watering. "I think that's cow manure!"

She stood there for a few minutes, letting her gaze roll over the property. The wraparound porch boasted a hanging swing at both ends. All along the front, hydrangeas with huge clusters of white, lavender, and pink blooms drew her toward them. She bent to push her nose in them, disappointment filling her at their lack of scent. From the look of them, she would think they would smell better than roses, but strangely, their hint of a scent was familiar to her.

She turned around and glanced at her father. "Do we know the people who live here? The house seems a little familiar."

"I've only met them once, and you've never met them," he answered, looking off toward the barn.

There was something he was keeping from her, and it made her stomach clench. She decided not to push him; it wasn't worth it. She was about to have to tell him goodbye for three entire months, and it was best if she tried to part on good terms. He irritated her, but she adored him; he'd always been a good father. Truthfully, this was really the only thing he'd ever asked her to do for him with such sincerity. Sure, he'd demanded that she finish college, but that didn't seem to mean as much to him as this, and she wondered why.

Was there really a lesson she was to learn before the summer was over? Whatever it was, she was betting it would be a hard lesson.

Two little girls came rambling out the door and stopped before descending the stairs of the porch when they saw Sophie. They were dressed in the same light blue dresses with white aprons, and their blond hair was twisted up and pinned behind their heads. Their bare feet were filthy, and their bright blue eyes stared at her. If not for one being a head taller than the other, she would have guessed they were twins.

"Hello," Sophie said timidly.

They ran back into the house.

Sophie turned around and shrugged at her father. "What did I do? Was I not supposed to talk to them?"

Hugh pointed to the front of the house where a man walked out with the little girls who stood close to him.

"It looks like they went inside to get their father."

"Mr. Yoder," her father said as he walked up to greet the man.

Sophie's breath hitched when he removed his hat revealing dark blonde hair. He was extremely handsome—not at all the way she'd pictured him. She'd expected an older man with a thick, scraggly beard hanging from his chin, but he was young and clean-shaven. She'd expected him to be dirty and unkempt in every way, but he was wearing a crisp blue dress shirt and black pants with suspenders. His black hat was sporty, and she thought it suited him. Had he gotten dressed up for their visit?

Sophie didn't know what to think of Mr. Yoder; she stood back and let her father converse with him. She couldn't take her eyes off him; was her father *really* going to let her live with this handsome man for three whole months? How was she going to get through the summer without giving away her attraction to him?

Her father turned around and beckoned her up to the porch. "This is Simon Yoder and his two daughters, Katie and Ellie."

Sophie extended a hand to Simon, not knowing how to greet him, but he didn't take her hand or shake it. She lowered it when he cast his eyes downward. He wouldn't even look at her! How was she going to live in this man's house if he wouldn't look at her or speak to her? Was that the Amish way?

She could only guess that as a woman she was not allowed to address him as a man.

Simon nodded curtly. "The *kinner* will take you in the *haus* to meet *mei mudder* and get you settled." Then he excused himself to Hugh and walked away.

Sophie hadn't really understood a word he'd said and wanted to jump back in the car and demand her father take her home immediately.

She leaned in toward her father and whispered while the little girls stood there and stared at her. "I can't stay here; that man doesn't want me here."

Hugh patted her arm. "He's a grieving widower; it might take him a little time to warm up to you."

The younger of the two girls approached her and tugged on her arm. Sophie looked down into her soulful eyes and smiled.

She smiled back and studied Sophie for a minute. "You look like *mei mamm!*"

Sophie turned to her dad and flashed him a look to help her out; she had no idea how to respond to such a comment.

"I have to go," her father said abruptly.

He hugged her rigid frame, and she whispered in his ear. "Dad, you can't leave me here like this— without an explanation!"

"You need to stay here," he reassured her. "Your mother would be proud."

Sophie pulled away from him and looked him in the eye. "She would? Why?"

"Stay here, and we'll talk when the summer is over," he said, his misty eyes clouding up with remorse.

Sophie stepped away from her father; her backpack slung over one shoulder; she was upset and unable to keep from feeling unwanted.

This is the End of this sample. If you enjoyed reading this extended sample, you can purchase a copy at the same retailer you purchased this book. Thank you for reading.

Blessings to you,

Samantha Bayarr